 use book
Random House Australia Pty Ltd
acific Highway, North Sydney NSW 2060
ouse.com.au

l by Random House in 2009

Dave Warner 2009

mpanies within the Random House Group can be found at
use.com.au/offices

of Australia
Publication Entry

Dave, 1953–
Hollywood / Dave Warner.
663 07 5 (pbk.)
Dave, 1953– Charlotte and the starlet 3
For primary school age.
– Juvenile fiction.
ood (Los Angeles, Calif.) – Juvenile fiction.
A823.3

saso content & design pty ltd
nd Typesetters, Australia
d by The SOS Print + Media Group

ustralia uses papers that are natural, renewable and recyclable
le from wood grown in sustainable forests. The logging
g processes are expected to conform to the environmental
country of origin.

Dave Warner is the author
fiction books for adults. He originally gained national
recognition as a musician and songwriter, with eight
albums to his name, but more recently music has been
secondary to Dave's career as a writer for television
and feature films.

www.davewarner.com.au
www.charlotteandthestarlet.com

Also by Dave Warner

Charlotte and the Starlet
Charlotte and the Starlet 2: A Friend in Need

CHARLOTTE AND THE Starlet

HOORAY
HOLLY

DAV

WIL

W

RANDOM HO

A Random Ho
Published by
Level 3, 100 F
www.random

First publishe

Copyright ©

The moral righ

Addresses for c
www.randomhd

National Librar
Cataloguing-in-

Author: Warner
Title: Hooray fo
ISBN: 978 1 741
Series: Warner,
Target audience:
Subjects: Schoo
Hollyw
Dewey Number:

Cover design by
Typeset by Midla
Printed and bour

Random House A
products and ma
and manufacturir
regulations of the

10 9 8 7 6 5 4 3

To my incredibly loyal supporter, Kate Ingleton, whose very generous donation has helped all those kids and families at Bear Cottage. Hooray for Hollywood, and three cheers for Kate.

Chapter 1

For the whole last week Charlotte had been in a state of nervous anticipation. As she prepared for her first-ever trip outside Australia, it was like being in the thick of a muster, with everything whirling around crazily. She was with Leila in her stables and it was the night before they were due to leave. In all her thirteen years she had never before had to concern herself too much with what to pack but she was in a quandary now. She realised that she had no idea what to expect from this trip to Hollywood.

Leila, a native of Los Angeles, was far more blasé. She chuckled.

'Light cotton T-shirts, jeans and a gasmask. L.A. is always sunny, warm and laden with smog.'

Charlotte didn't have a gasmask. Jeans and her one and only summer dress would have to do.

Leila shifted on her four hooves, coughed in that long equine throat of hers and said, 'Aren't you forgetting something?'

Her nose flicked a brush off the stable peg. It landed on Charlotte's bag.

'They'll have lots of brushes for me to do your coat.'

'Yes, but that's my favourite.'

Charlotte grunted and packed the brush. It would be her job to groom and exercise Leila while they shot the movie. They would be staying at the house of Joel Gold, the producer. He had a stable and vast grounds where they could exercise. Leila had explained to Charlotte that, as producer, it was Mr Gold's job to make sure the film was made for the amount it was supposed to cost. The movie studio actually supplied the money but Mr Gold was the one who decided how it was spent. He oversaw everything from the script to the finished film.

Leila observed, 'And, by the way, this time of the year the nights can get a little chilly by the pool unless you're right next to the Tahitian torches, so pack a cardigan. There are a few things I need you to get for my pals too.'

'Like what?'

'I want you to find Feathers some real Australian gumleaves for his cage.'

Feathers was the talking parrot Leila had hung out with before winding up in Australia. 'And a snow dome for my pal, Paris.'

'The branch I can do. Maybe I can buy a snow dome at the airport.'

'Good. And a jar of fire ants, please.'

That pulled Charlotte up. 'Fire ants?'

'To liberally sprinkle over Sarah-Jane.'

Sarah-Jane Sweeney was Leila's young co-star. The two had an intense rivalry.

'No way. No fire ants.'

'Come on, it's Hollywood. Everybody loves to see their co-star in pain,' Leila pleaded.

'So I wonder what Sarah-Jane has in mind for you?' Charlotte fired back.

Leila mused a moment before coming back strongly. 'You're absolutely right. I definitely need those fire ants!'

'You're not going to get them. I'm off to bed.'

'Fancy a game of hang the man first?'

'We're leaving at the crack of dawn so I'm going to bed now. I'll see you in the morning.'

'We're going to have fun, Charlie.'

'I hope so.'

Charlotte kissed Leila and headed outside. She snapped a small branch off a gum tree for Feathers and returned to her room where her roommate, Hannah, was waiting.

'Remember to take a camera,' said Hannah. 'On the set of a Hollywood movie you'll probably get lots of opportunities to snap stars.'

'I might if I had one.'

'Take mine.'

Charlotte tried to resist but Hannah was insistent. It inspired Charlotte to add her autograph book, just in case. It was still relatively empty. So far she only had entries from her father, another stockman, John Patcher, Mr Jedley, the chemist at Goondowi, and Hannah. As she and Miss Strudworth were staying at Mr Gold's, Charlotte thought there might be an opportunity to get the autograph of a famous actor. Charlotte wasn't sure if Russ Raven or Frangelina De Fontaine lived near Mr Gold but her dad was a huge fan of both actors so she thought she should give it a shot.

By the time she crammed a cardigan, riding boots and helmet in, as well as the gum leaves for Feathers, her backpack was looking like Leila's stomach after a pizza pig-out.

Charlotte hardly slept she was so excited. Hannah was still fast asleep when Charlotte rose and dressed, grabbed her things and headed for the stable. Dawn was just breaking as she led a sleepy Leila to the horse float. Miss Strudworth was waiting at the car, bright-eyed.

'Ready for our big adventure, Richards?'

'I hope so.'

'Me too. This is the future of Thornton Downs,' said Strudworth gravely. The fee from Leila's performance in the film would help Miss Strudworth pay off a law suit from the father of Lucinda Hayes-Warrington, one of the stuck-up princesses of the Junior Olympic Equestrian Squad to which Charlotte belonged. Lucinda had broken her collarbone and thanks to Miss Strudworth's inept nephew Chadwick, Thornton Downs had not been covered by insurance. Lucinda's father had claimed that her future had been threatened. Charlotte didn't quite see how. As far as she could tell Lucinda's future didn't extend beyond which dress to buy next.

The car trip was long and it was afternoon by the time they reached the city. First they had to locate the freight area at the airport to unload Leila. She was not pleased to discover she wasn't travelling on the same plane as Charlotte and Miss Strudworth.

'You have to travel in a special cargo plane,' Charlotte explained.

'Why?'

'Look at the size of you. They would have to take out too many seats.'

'Mr Gold will pay.'

Leila could be very stubborn, but Charlotte had a way around that – flattery.

'You need special padding so that magnificent coat of yours doesn't get scratched.'

That seemed to appease Leila.

'Okay, but am I travelling first class cargo or coach cargo?'

Charlotte was pretty sure there was no difference in cargo but she had been with Leila long enough to know it wasn't worth giving her the chance to complain.

'First class, of course. Strudworth and I are both in economy.'

'What's that got to do with anything? I'm the star. I'm the one that Joel Gold is prepared to pay a million bucks to have in his movie.'

Charlotte could see through Leila's attitude. 'You're scared.'

'Damn right I'm scared. Hollywood changes real quick. What if I'm not hip any more?'

Charlotte draped her arms around Leila's neck. 'You'll still be my friend.'

Leila calmed. 'Yeah. You'll be mine too . . .' she added, 'especially if you've got those fire ants.'

'No fire ants. Sorry.'

That was all they had time to say before the attendants came and loaded Leila on the cargo plane.

It was another half hour before they parked and entered the airport terminal, which seemed as big as all of the cattle pens in Snake Hills put together. Charlotte's heavy backpack threatened to topple her but she trudged past the ticket counters of numerous airlines doggedly in pursuit of the long-striding Miss Strudworth. Strudworth pushed her own heavily laden trolley, with seeming ease, across the acres of gleaming linoleum, turning every thirty seconds or so to urge Charlotte to keep up.

'Come on, Charlotte, once we check in we can relax.'

Though their plane would not leave for an hour or so, they would arrive at Los Angeles Airport around the same time as Leila. Charlotte was feeling really tired now. They finally stopped in front of a counter.

'Passport.' Strudworth flipped out her hand. Charlotte had kept the passport close to her heart. Both her father and Strudworth had warned her not to let it out of her sight. The butterflies in her stomach were building as she tried not to think too much about being in a plane high in the sky. Hannah had told her what to expect, giving a detailed run-down on how you operated the entertainment device in your seat. She also advised Charlotte to get to the toilet before the trays of food came out or she would be trapped. Charlotte was handing over the passport, allowing Miss Strudworth to give the airline clerk their details, when a familiar voice sounded behind her.

'Ready for L.A., Charlotte?'

Todd Greycroft stood there with a broad grin. She could hardly speak.

'Todd?'

She was thrilled he had come all the way here to see her off but confused too. Todd was in the boys Junior Olympic Equestrian Squad, which was located on the adjoining property to Thornton Downs. He should have been training or in school, not taking the day off.

'Won't you get into trouble?'

He smiled, showing white, even teeth. 'I'm riding in competition in San Diego. It's only a couple of hours drive from Los Angeles.'

'Wow! How long has that been on the cards?'

'A while now. I thought I'd keep it a surprise. The competition only goes for a week so we might be able to catch up in Los Angeles before I fly home.'

Charlotte was excited by the idea of having another friend to hang out with in Los Angeles.

'Unfortunately we're not on the same airline.' Todd had guessed what she was thinking.

'Oh,' Charlotte felt a pang of disappointment.

'But after a few hours you really just want to sleep anyway.'

Todd was from a wealthy family and flying was second nature to him.

Miss Strudworth turned from the counter and smiled at Todd.

'Mr Greycroft, you are in the Del Mar competition, I believe?'

'That's right.'

'Good luck.'

'They're all good riders. I'll need it.'

Todd glanced over, saw his team leader gesturing to him and announced he had better be off. Charlotte told him where they were staying and Todd announced he would be in touch, then he left to join his team. Strudworth checked her watch.

'I believe we have time for a hot chocolate before we board. Would you like that, Charlotte?'

Charlotte did not have to be asked twice. She followed the lanky Strudworth, pleased she would have time to write her dad a card from the airport. He'd been even more excited than her that she had the opportunity of travelling overseas. Looking at Strudworth, Charlotte couldn't help feeling slightly guilty. For Charlotte, this trip was something of an adventure, but for Miss Strudworth it was everything.

Under the agreement she had with Mr Gold, not a cent would be paid until Leila's role in the movie was complete. The possibility that something might go wrong sent a chill down Charlotte's spine but she shrugged it off quickly. Nothing would go wrong. Leila would arrive and do the movie, Miss Strudworth would be paid and they could all live happily ever after. And right now she would enjoy every sip of a thick, creamy, hot chocolate . . .

. . . with four marshmallows. Leila woke from the dream in which she had been stretched out poolside at the Four Seasons Hotel, guest of the movie studio with unlimited spend on their credit account. It was that 'unlimited spend' that alerted her to it being a dream. The studios were never *that* generous. She blinked at her dark and noisy surrounds. It took her a moment to recollect she was in the cargo hold of a plane heading across the Pacific back to her homeland.

The tingle of fear started again.

It was crazy. She knew there was nobody in Hollywood who was a bigger draw than her . . . well, at the time she had been nag-napped by those bumbling criminals and somehow wound up in Australia, there had been nobody bigger. But like she'd told Charlotte, Hollywood moved a lot faster than a sushi-train. Apart from Clint Eastwood and Mike Myers, nobody stayed big in Hollywood for long. Mr Gold's last film with Sarah-Jane had been a flop and the studio who financed the film had not been happy. Leila liked to think the film had failed because she wasn't in it, but what if time had simply moved on? What if she'd become old news like *The Nanny*, pet rocks or those Japanese tama-watchemecallits that kids nurtured like children?

Leila forced herself to calm down. She had to get that negativity out of her head. Her friends, Charlotte and Miss Strudworth, were counting on her. Besides, it wasn't all bad. While she was on set she'd get a complimentary massage between takes. And the caterers did those delicious mini pizzas.

Her eyes having grown accustomed to the dark, she realised she was in a padded stall but not alone in the hold. She could smell some foul feline that had peed in its cage. From her position she could see just far enough over the padded wall to spy three dogs in cages on the other side of the plane but her nose told her that she was also in the presence of other horses. She couldn't see them or make out what they were muttering in horse but she knew they were there.

'Who are you guys?' she called out in Horswegian, which, to the other animals or human ears, sounded like a long whinny.

A deep, resonant male voice came back.

'I don't believe it. Leila?'

'Warrior? Is that you?'

It was a stupid question. Warrior, Todd Greycroft's competition mount, was a dark hunk of a stallion, and nobody but nobody had the pipes that boy did. Not that Leila would ever let him know it. He was conceited enough as it was. Leila and he had begun as enemies but when Leila had been trapped by some bad dudes logging illegally in a nature reserve and Warrior had done his bit to help with her rescue, a little two-way flirtation had been on the menu. Unfortunately ever since, the boy and girl JOES had been flat out training or doing schoolwork. Todd hadn't crossed paths with Charlotte much and therefore Warrior and Leila had seen little of one another. Warrior's mellifluous voice floated from the dark, allowing Leila to pinpoint his yellow eyes.

'Yeah, it's me. You competing in San Diego too?'

'I'm doing a movie. The old babe who runs Thornton Downs is being sued and they need me to earn some cash.'

'Very altruistic of you.'

She picked up a hint of cynicism in his voice.

'Hey, I'm on the level,' she said, a little offended.

'Good to hear it. I like the new Leila a lot more than the old, selfish, prima donna who couldn't even speak Horswegian.'

'I could speak horse; I just chose not to.'

Leila thanked her lucky stars it was so dark in here. Her mane was matted, her tail was limp and the moisturiser Charlotte had applied to her muzzle had evaporated. Not the circumstances a girl wanted to be seen by a hot stallion.

'So tell us about the movie. What happens?'

'Wish I knew. It's all been kind of a rush and I haven't seen a script yet.'

'So you don't know if it's any good.'

'It'll be good. Honey Grace has written all my movies and she's a really good writer. The script is the least of my worries.'

Fifteen years ago, at the age of twenty-six, Honey Grace had arrived in Hollywood from her small home town in Pennsylvania where she had been quite successful in writing for local theatre. She had started doing the rounds to find work as a screenwriter and realised very soon that first she needed an agent. But no agent wanted to take on yet another out-of-work writer so she had worked as a sales assistant at a second-hand clothing store while entering every script competition she could find. Nothing happened for her. At the age of thirty-three, after seven long years of frustration, she gave up her notion of ever being a screenwriter.

And then Oscar entered her life.

Oscar was a large ginger tomcat who she had found foraging near her apartment block. Actually back then, Oscar was a wee kitten, but wild; hence the name Oscar after Honey Grace's favourite playwright, Oscar Wilde, not after the statuette that dominated so many Hollywood thoughts year in and year out. Oscar began to take food from her but always maintained a safe distance until, one day, he followed her back to her apartment where he had stayed ever since. Apparently Oscar had deemed her worthy of sheltering him. The day after Oscar's arrival she had received a phone call from a producer named Joel Gold. He had been a judge on a competition she had entered and felt her writing would perfectly suit a little movie he was doing about a girl and her horse. Oscar had brought with him a change in fortune. Honey Grace wrote *Thrills and Spills*, the first of the hit movies starring Leila and Sarah-Jane. *Dressage To Kill* and more hits followed until that dreadful incident where Leila had been kidnapped. Unfortunately the most recent of the movies she had written for Mr Gold had lacked the chemistry Leila brought to the screen. It had not been successful and Honey was considering perhaps now was the time to try that novel she had always wanted to write. Then last month Mr Gold had contacted her and asked her to have a script ready for Leila's return. Honey had been very excited at the prospect of writing again for Leila and Sarah-Jane, and with Oscar curled up beside her, she quickly hit her stride, tapping away at her computer, creating a fun adventure in which Leila and Sarah-Jane would defeat a wildlife smuggling operation and Leila would wind up being elected Governor of California.

Everything was going smoothly. She was already nearly a third of the way there and though the deadline was tight, she had no doubt she would finish the screenplay in time.

She banged on the tin of tuna fish, expecting Oscar to hurtle in from the balcony where he loved to sun himself. Oscar did not appear. She banged again.

Still no Oscar.

Honey took herself out to her balcony and looked for him. He wasn't there. She could have sworn that's where he'd been this morning but possibly she'd been too engrossed in her writing to notice him slip out. Oscar would often prowl the halls of the apartment building looking for the odd tickle or treat from the other tenants. Honey opened the door to the hallway expecting to see Oscar waiting on the mat. Nope, not there either. She wasn't perturbed. When he was hungry Oscar would return. In the meantime she had best get on with her story. Perhaps she should have a scene where Sarah-Jane rode Leila into the White House? Maybe dress Sarah-Jane as George Washington? That could be fun.

ɔ ɔ ɔ ɔ

Fun, it was going to be real fun.

You couldn't see it in the dark of the cargo hold, but Leila had a smile the size of Texas on her face as she thought about what awaited that painful and precocious Sarah-Jane. The brat who loved to dig her boot heels into Leila unnecessarily, who always insisted on a bigger trailer, would get her come-uppance big time. Leila had not been surprised that Charlotte had declined to assist her in what was a necessary part of establishing the pecking order on any film shoot. The kid was too nice. Leila just had to do it herself as best she could. She shut her eyes again. Only another nine hours to LAX, glazed doughnuts and that wonderful smog.

Apart from that moment when the jet accelerated and first lifted off the runway, and later on a few bumps that had her swivelling to see if the flight attendants looked worried, Charlotte was fine. Looking out of the window, seeing the city far below like some Lego town, was actually fun. While Miss Strudworth snored beside her, Charlotte tried to watch the movie on the little screen on the back of the seat in front of her. It wasn't easy. The problem was Giles, the boy in front. He was an A-grade pain. As soon as Giles had got on the plane it had started. He had opened the luggage locker above and thrust a bunch of heavy tourist purchases right onto Charlotte's small personal bag. His items included a mass-produced set of boomerangs, a miniature Uluru – although still clearly heavy from the way he strained to get it up there – and a carved wooden kangaroo. He then sat down with the grace of a concrete block hitting a footpath. Charlotte immediately checked her bag to find the delicate papier-mâché model of the Sydney Harbour Bridge she had bought for Mr Gold was crushed flat, and the snow dome she had bought for Leila's friend Paris was cracked. Fortunately Hannah's camera was still intact. A packet that, apparently, contained tea bags, which Charlotte assumed Miss Strudworth must have slipped into her bag, had also been battered.

Giles spent the next two hours whining for treats from his mother but whatever she handed over didn't satisfy him. From the look of Giles a forced diet wouldn't have done any harm. He was constantly reclining his seat then sitting it upright, then reclining it again, and he hit the attendant button every five minutes, asking for more soft drink. He played some video game so loudly that even with the volume on her earphones up high, Charlotte had trouble hearing the movie. Mercifully, he seemed to grow tired when they turned out the cabin lights and Charlotte had fifteen minutes of uninterrupted viewing pleasure. Sadly, it didn't last. He was now twisting and turning in his seat. It seemed to be contagious. His mother was beginning to jerk around quite violently. What was going on?

Charlotte took out her earphones and now she could hear Giles and his mother muttering and moaning.

'Ow, youch!' cried the woman.

'Something's biting me!' yelled the annoying Giles.

Good, thought Charlotte, payback.

Giles reached up and pressed the attendant button. Since the plane had gone dark no attendants had been by. Charlotte wouldn't blame them keeping a wide berth from Giles.

By now Giles was out of his seat and stomping. Passengers across the aisle began a similar ritual. Soon at least a dozen people were in various stages of wriggling distress and attendant call buttons were going off everywhere.

It was then that Charlotte looked across at the sleeping Strudworth. Her mouth was agape, her nose pointing at the ceiling. And right on the tip of that nose was a wart . . . a moving, red wart. Charlotte craned closer for a better look.

It couldn't be what she thought it was . . . what on earth would a fire ant be doing on a plane?

Her heart seized. Her eyes travelled up towards the luggage compartment above her head. Even in the dim light she could discern the moving mass and the trail sneaking its way to all areas of the plane.

Leila!!!!!!

Now, everywhere, people were shrieking and whacking their legs, doing crazy dances. Attendants were converging on the scene but hadn't reached the epicentre of the problem, as passengers on the perimeter seized them first.

'I want help,' yelled Giles.

Nobody seemed to have noticed yet where the ants were coming from. It was not in Charlotte's nature to be deceptive, nor to shy from whatever punishment was duly hers, but on this occasion she made an exception. With everybody else distracted she opened the locker. Sure enough the ant colony appeared to be streaming from the tea packet in her bag. Clearly it had *not* been placed there by Miss Strudworth but by a certain sneaky quadruped named Leila. Charlotte's eyes expanded to the size of golf balls. There were still as many ants in the box as had already left it. Out of the corner of her eye she saw the head flight attendant arrive. She did the only thing a sensible girl could. She bravely took the box and shoved it inside the pouch of Giles' wooden kangaroo. Then she shut the compartment, brushed a couple of stray ants from herself and resumed her seat. All around the cabin, attendants in masks were hastily fumigating.

The stern flight attendant sprayed Giles all over. Giles protested loudly.

'Poo, that stinks, that's making my eyes water, it's making my tongue swell . . .'

The flight attendant looked as though he would be delighted if Giles' tongue kept swelling and choked him.

'I'm trying to help you,' said the attendant. 'It appears there are fire ants on the plane.'

Giles' mother announced that it was appalling. She was going to contact the media. That inspired Giles.

'I'll put it on my blog.'

Yeah, big readership, I'll bet, thought Charlotte.

'The airline should refund the fares,' added the mother.

The flight attendant declared that prior to embarkation the aircraft had been free of any 'pests'. He shot a close look at Giles as he said this, implying Giles himself belonged in that category.

The word 'embarkation' clearly stumped Giles. He wrinkled up his nose and grunted, 'Huh?'

The flight attendant translated. 'The ants were brought on by a passenger.'

Giles' mother opined the offending passenger should be given a parachute and shoved out of the plane. It was at that moment the attendant noted the ants streaming from the locker.

He lifted the locker and surveyed the scene. Charlotte's pulse was racing. Fortunately Miss Strudworth was still snoring.

'Hmm. Think I've found the culprit,' said the attendant, bringing out the wooden kangaroo. 'Who does this belong to?'

Charlotte watched many pairs of angry eyes focus on the scene. Giles went as red as a beetroot and stammered, 'That's . . . mine.'

His mother shot a withering look at him. The flight attendant said, 'I am afraid I will have to destroy this item.'

The mother looked ashamed.

'And in future your names will be placed on a watch list. You'll have to arrive early before check-in so the contents of your baggage can be thoroughly investigated.'

The other passengers clapped.

The flight attendant was emboldened. 'Would you like me to fetch that parachute for your son, madam?'

Giles' mother apologised profusely for the actions of her 'nitwit' son. Giles shrank visibly. The total humiliation of Giles had Charlotte grinning from ear to ear. It almost made it worth sparing Leila a lecture.

Chapter 2

By the time the plane landed and Charlotte and Miss Strudworth had made it through immigration, nearly twenty-four hours had passed since leaving Australia. Charlotte estimated she'd had three hours sleep, tops. Her head felt foggy, her feet slow. Miss Strudworth, on the other hand, had slept almost the entire time and seemed quite sparky. They reclaimed their luggage and emerged through big swing doors into the arrivals area. Charlotte's eyes immediately fell on a plump man with a round face and thinning hair. This was Joel Gold. Waving effusively, he called them over.

'Charlotte, Caroline.' He shook their hands warmly. 'My chauffeur, Fernando, will take your luggage.'

He indicated a man with a very neat moustache and wearing an immaculate uniform. Fernando bowed to them.

'Pleased to meet you, ladies.'

Mr Gold was already barrelling towards the exit, enquiring after their flight.

'Uneventful, really,' said Strudworth, who remained ignorant of the fire-ant episode. They pushed out of the arrivals hall into a warm day. Charlotte was so excited to think she was actually in America! Mr Gold was telling her he had passes for her to Excelsior Studios, the makers of the Leila movies, and also Universal Studios and Disneyland.

'Anywhere you want to sightsee, Fernando and the car are at your disposal.'

Car was an understatement. Charlotte gaped at the size of the shiny black limousine. It seemed about half the length of the plane they had just got off. Fernando loaded their luggage into the boot as Joel Gold held the door open for them.

'Leila's plane is touching down now at the freight area. We'll go straight there.'

ↄ ↄ ↄ ↄ

Leila felt the wheels touch down and bump across the tarmac. She was home sweet home and part of her felt like dancing on the ceiling. The other part, however, was not ready to celebrate. The anxiety that had slipped away during the flight began to creep up through her hooves again. Maybe this was a bad mistake. Perhaps she should have stayed in Australia, kept working on the jumping game? There was nothing worse than a starlet who didn't know her use-by date.

The plane came to a halt.

'Good luck on the movie,' called Warrior in Horswegian.

'You too with the equestrian competition.'

She felt a pang deep inside. It would have been so much easier in so many ways if she and Charlotte were just over here to jump. Now there's something she never would have thought before. One consolation would be teaming up with her parrot pal, Feathers. He had been her best friend for so long. In fact only he and Charlotte knew her most closely guarded secret: she could speak human. Mr Gold, the director Tommy Tempest and even Sarah-Jane all thought she was just a horse smart enough to read their body cues. Leila was happy to let them think that. She had no desire to wind up in some laboratory, being ogled by a bunch of egghead scientists. If there was any prodding and jabbing to be done, she preferred to leave that to the studio masseur!

There was a rumbling and a clanking of chains as the back of the plane lowered and light streamed in.

People in overalls entered. Leila was finally able to see Warrior. Lord, that was a handsome coat stretched over those taut muscles! A handler slipped on a bridle and began to lead her out. She looked back and nodded at Warrior. He threw his head around, blew through his nostrils and whinnied loudly. Translated, he'd just told her to break a leg. She assumed he meant it in the theatrical way.

Leila started down the steel walkway. After so many hours in the dark, the light was blinding. But even though it forced her eyes shut, she was able to smell that wonderful odour of thick smog mixed with gasoline, Eau de L.A. Her reverie was interrupted by screaming.

'There she is!'

'It's Leila.'

'Welcome home, babe.'

Leila flicked open her eyes to find a sizeable crowd gathered behind barriers. There were people of all ages – mainly young girls in Leila T-shirts and caps but older men and women too. Flashes erupted as people took pictures of their favourite star. Whatever anxiety she felt was exterminated. Leila drank in the adulation, the whistles, the applause – ah, just how she remembered it, only sweeter now. She found an extra inch or two by straightening her neck to the max, and strutted towards the bunched media giving her biggest and brightest smile for the TV cameras from *Entertainment Tonight*.

'I think she's slimmer than before,' remarked one reporter.

Leila did a model half-turn, giving the cameras a nice shot of her firm butt. She preened, offering the other cheek, smiling a coquettish smile. It felt good to be a star. Suddenly there was movement among the media. They began to split apart, the cameras spun away from Leila.

'Excuse me, ladies and gentlemen, let Sarah-Jane through, please.'

Bodyguards, who looked like something out of the President's secret service squad, ushered forward the diminutive figure of Sarah-Jane Sweeney. Leila's coquettish smile evolved into a sneer. The little vixen was upstaging her return! How Leila wished she had that packet of fire ants. Sarah-Jane's people pushed aside the barrier and she ran and draped an arm around Leila's neck. Fake tears spluttered from her eyes. A hundred cameras clicked.

'Leila, you gorgeous girl, have you missed me?' gasped Sarah-Jane. Leila recognised the line from *Hot to Trot*, their fourth movie. Sarah-Jane said it with exactly the same inflection.

'Like a nail in my hoof,' Leila wanted to answer.

The competitiveness had begun already. Sarah-Jane couldn't even let Leila have a small moment of glory, she had to horn in. Leila tried to stomp on her foot but Sarah-Jane was too quick and stepped out of the way.

'Look everybody, Leila wants to dance with me.'

Sighs filled the air. Leila gritted her teeth. Where were those fire ants when you needed them?

ʊ ʊ ʊ ʊ

Charlotte and Miss Strudworth followed Mr Gold through the crowd. Charlotte immediately recognised the girl with her arm around Leila's neck as Sarah-Jane. She could imagine what Leila thought about that. Sarah-Jane might be Charlotte's age but she was wearing make-up and was clearly used to cameras and crowds. Mr Gold ushered Miss Strudworth through the barriers. Charlotte went to follow but felt the firm hand of one of Sarah-Jane's security people on her chest.

'Stay outside the barrier, miss.'

Charlotte didn't know what to do. Joel Gold and Strudworth were already striding on without her. She felt a sudden stab of disappointment as she looked over to see Leila with Sarah-Jane joined moments later by Mr Gold and Miss Strudworth. For the first time it occurred to Charlotte that maybe this would not be a fun time with Leila, and worse, that Leila, once back in the world of show business, might want to stay.

Leila was settling in to a rhythm now. The cameras came in for close-ups and she hammed it up, fluttering her eyelids the way she did in the movies whenever they gave her a 'love interest' – invariably some wussy white gelding named Lightning. She even did the old arabesque for them, a relatively simple manoeuvre that required her to stretch and hold her near side foreleg off the ground at the same time as her off-side hind leg.

'Aaaaah,' she heard the crowd gasp. One of Sarah-Jane's assistants handed over a magnificent chocolate cake that Sarah-Jane held out towards Leila.

'Welcome back, my beautiful friend,' smiled Sarah-Jane, her eyes not on Leila but the TV cameras. Leila had a good mind to bunt her . . . but that chocolate cake did look tempting and after such a long flight with nothing but chaff . . .

She was just about to take a chomp when she noticed Joel Gold and Strudworth out of the corner of her eye. But where was Charlotte? She swivelled her head and caught sight of her behind a barrier. What was Charlie doing there? Leila broke away from Sarah-Jane and galloped towards Charlie. She wasn't even aware of the crowd's panic. She just wanted to see her pal. The barriers were about the height of a man's chest. Nothing compared to what Leila had been jumping at Thornton Downs. She launched herself and cleared it easily.

Charlotte witnessed Leila's charge towards her. She's not going to, she told herself. Surely not. But as people scattered left and right shrieking in fear, she knew exactly what was going to happen next. Leila leapt the barrier, landed beside her and shoved her head in her chest.

'What are you doing back here like nancy no-friends?' Leila whispered so nobody could hear.

'I'm just your groom.'

'No, you're my best friend.'

Reassured that Leila was no threat, fans and media came flooding back as quickly as they had left.

'Who's the girl?'

'Who are you, honey?' asked a young woman who looked like a bigger version of Hannah's Barbie doll.

Leila nudged Charlottte in the back, sending her towards the reporters.

'Um, I'm Charlotte.'

Witnessing this from the other side of the barrier, Sarah-Jane was not impressed. In fact she was livid. Who was this upstart? She hurled the cake away in disgust.

The forklift driver was trying not to pay too much attention to the crowd. Apparently some famous horse was arriving but it didn't mean all that much to him except extra hazards on the runway. He had picked up a crate from the hold of the cargo plane that was depositing Leila and was heading to the customs building when some dark sticky mass flew through the air and smashed into his face. Had he known it was chocolate cake he might have felt less threatened and perhaps would not have lost control of the forklift. But all he knew was one minute he could see, the next minute it was black. He reached up to gouge the stuff from his eyes. The forklift veered, striking a stationary baggage trolley.

Charlotte heard the loud crunch and turned with the rest of the crowd, to see the forklift merged and

31

tangled with what a moment before had been a large baggage trolley. The damage was not major but the crate that had been on the forklift, labelled WILDLIFE PARK, toppled and fell, splintering apart on impact with the tarmac. Leila was among the many who burst into spontaneous laughter. It was one of those stupidly funny incidents hard not to laugh at. Very quickly, however, the laughter turned to frightened shrieks. People seemed a lot more scared than they had a few minutes before when Leila had leapt towards them. The Barbie look-alike reporter saw the reason for the sudden panic.

'Snakes!' she yelled. She turned to flee but her six-inch stiletto heel snapped and she toppled into her camera crew, who proceeded to fall into more people behind them. Charlotte's father often relaxed by making a house of cards and the effect was not unlike when one of them started to crumple. People toppled, causing those in front and behind to fall as well. To accentuate the problem the horses travelling with Warrior found snakes slithering towards them and began rearing. One broke free and ran to the back of the crowd of fans. What had been a lovely homecoming for Leila had degenerated into a potential disaster.

One thing that did not alarm Charlotte was a snake

– poisonous or otherwise. Her hometown had earned the name Snake Hills because its hills literally did teem with snakes and Charlotte had been playing with them since she was a toddler. Leila, on the other hand, was a horse. Snakes scared her even more than a first-time make-up artist.

'Snakes!!!' She reared reflexively. That didn't help matters.

Charlotte could see people at the front of the barriers who had fallen were in danger of being smothered by those behind. Grabbing a sound boom that had hit the ground when the frightened operator had fled with a speed that suggested he was by now halfway to San Diego, Charlotte vaulted the barrier and strode towards the mass of squirming reptiles. She recognised them all pretty much immediately. Most were harmless but there were king browns, dugites and taipans, which could all kill a person with their poison. Using the boom handle, she circled the perimeter of the writhing mass, scooping the dangerous ones back into the pile whenever they tried to break free.

A policeman screamed in on his motorcycle and drew his gun, attempting to get a bead on the reptiles Charlotte allowed to flee.

'Those ones are harmless,' yelled Charlotte. She

needed something to cover the poisonous ones pronto. Her eyes spied a limp banner, which, when extended between two poles, read 'Love U Leila' with the U in the shape of a horseshoe.

'Give me that banner. Now!!!'

The teenage girls holding it were too scared to refuse. They threw the banner over the barrier.

'Help me,' Charlotte yelled to the motorcycle cop, indicating he bring her the banner. The cop looked extremely apprehensive but did as he was told.

'You take that end, and on the count of three we drop it, right?'

They each took one of the wooden poles. She couldn't look at the cop because one spritely taipan had almost broken free. Charlotte had to dance over it before sliding it back like a hockey puck.

'One, two . . . three.'

They dropped the banner over the poisonous snakes, the poles providing enough weight on each of their sides to trap them at least momentarily. Charlotte quickly placed the boom across the third side of the moving canvas rectangle. That left only one side the serpents could attempt to escape from. That exit was quickly eliminated by some airport workers carrying one of the crowd barriers and placing it on that edge of the banner.

'That should hold them,' observed Charlotte calmly. A loud piercing scream split the air. Charlotte turned to find Sarah-Jane standing on the saddle of the policeman's bike.

'It's trying to kill me,' she screamed.

'If only,' thought Leila, who had watched proudly as Charlotte wrangled the snakes. Now she saw Charlotte advance towards the shrieking Sarah-Jane, bend down and pluck the offending snake by its tail.

'It's a python. Only dangerous if you're a rat,' said Charlotte, trying to reassure Sarah-Jane.

'What if you're a brat?' quipped Leila, in the safety of the crowd. Loud chuckles erupted around her.

Charlotte picked up the python and draped it over her shoulders. The crowd burst into applause. Sarah-Jane turned red.

'Three cheers for the snake girl,' yelled somebody in the crowd.

'Crocodoll Dundee lives,' called somebody else.

The Barbie reporter and her crew were already racing towards Charlotte, who was totally surprised by the reaction.

Clambering down from the police bike and watching the crowd mob the interloper, Sarah-Jane felt humiliated. And very angry. Her manager, who had been watching events from the safety of his

Porsche, surmised that the danger had passed and hurried over.

'You all right, Sarah?'

Sarah-Jane's eyes narrowed at Charlotte receiving adulation.

'I better be,' she snarled, 'or you're down one very important client.'

Leila trotted to Charlotte's side, making sure the cameras got her best profile. Joel Gold was holding court.

'. . . all the way from the outback. She's Leila's equestrian rider and groom. And this is Leila's owner, the marvellous Caroline Strudworth.'

Strudworth shyly nodded to the multitude.

'Is Leila your favourite horse?' somebody asked.

Strudworth preened.

'I had a wonderful jumper, Zucchini . . .'

The reporters were in for a very long session. Leila surveyed the scene: Charlotte, with a dozen microphones shoved in her face; Joel Gold, working the moment for maximum potential; and even Miss Strudworth having her fifteen minutes of fame.

L.A. You had to love it!

Chapter 3

'Don't you ever try a stunt like that again. What if the ants had got into the cockpit and attacked the pilots? The plane could have crashed.'

'*Your* plane could have crashed,' Leila chuckled.

'Not funny.'

Leila purred. 'Come on, Charlie, aren't we being a tad dramatic? Kick back, look around you.'

Charlotte couldn't help but do just that, taking in the magnificent manicured lawns of Mr Gold's estate. They looked like acres of green felt, too neat to walk on. Leila and Charlotte were currently walking the perimeter of a fabulous fifty-metre swimming pool; its brilliant blue surface far more stunning than the smudgy sky overhead. A row of hedge-type bushes that had been clipped into the shape of the Oscar statuette surrounded the pool, offering them enough privacy for quiet conversation.

Leila sighed wistfully at what had once been her everyday surrounds.

'This is the land where we turn dreams into money.'

'You disobey me again and it'll be the land where I turn horse into hamburger!'

'Ouch!' Leila giggled. She nudged Charlotte with her muzzle.

'Come on, I'm sorry, okay? You saw what Sarah-Jane was like. Trying to shoe-horn in on my moment of glory.' Leila perfectly mocked Sarah-Jane's voice, '"Oh look, Leila wants to dance with me." I wanted to dance all right, all over her stupid fat head.'

'Sarah-Jane?'

A man's voice came from behind one of the herbaceous Oscars. Charlotte threw a nervous look at Leila, who whispered, 'Tommy Tempest.'

Charlotte knew Tommy was the director of Leila's films. She had seen him when he had come to Australia to collect Leila. On that occasion Leila had bitten him and Joel Gold in a ploy to get them to leave her at Thornton Downs. Tommy emerged from around the bush. He was a freckly faced, sandy-haired man and was on crutches. His face registered surprise.

'Oh, hi. Charlotte, right?'

'Yes. Hello, Mr Tempest.'

'Saw you on the TV. Nice job with those snakes. Hi Leila.'

Leila moved over to give Tommy a big lick but wary from the last time he'd encountered her, he moved backwards, too quickly for his limited expertise with crutches, and fell in a heap.

'Ah. Darn things.'

Charlotte helped him up.

'Thank you.'

'I'm sure Leila won't bite you again. Will you, Leila?'

As Tommy regained his balance, Leila nuzzled him gently.

'Thank goodness for that. Wouldn't want to be spending the next five weeks with a psychotic animal.' Leila was tempted to mention he'd be doing just that with Sarah-Jane. Tommy's brow creased and he looked about him. 'Did I hear Sarah-Jane before?'

Charlotte improvised. 'Actually, that was me.'

Tommy was impressed. 'Really? Wow. It sounded just like her. Do it again . . .'

Charlotte was saved from disaster by approaching voices. She looked over to see Joel Gold with Miss Strudworth and two men in suits.

'My goodness, Tommy, what happened?' asked the taller of the two men. He was grey-haired and about Mr Gold's age.

'Accident on the lot, Mr Martinez. Somebody driving a golf cart ran into me.'

Martinez turned to the other newcomer. 'Fired the culprit I presume, Hawthorn?'

Hawthorn was thin with short, jet-black hair. 'I would if I could find him. It was a hit and run.'

Martinez shook his head sadly. 'It could have been a terrible disaster.'

Tommy said, 'Luckily it was only a bone in my foot.'

Martinez waved that away, 'No, I mean it could have delayed the movie. We're on schedule, Joel, right?'

Mr Gold nodded strenuously. 'Yes, Hector.'

Hector Martinez visibly relaxed. Charlotte noted that he shared that anxious look her father got when there were cattle missing from the herd.

'That's what I want to hear. I don't need to tell you I'm under pressure from the board. If we have a setback, well, I could be out of a job and there'd be no guarantee the new studio boss would bankroll your film.'

'No guarantee at all,' offered Hawthorn in a show of solidarity.

'I'm on very shaky ground,' added Hector.

'. . . hanging by a thread,' said Hawthorn.

Hector shot him a sharp look. 'Let's not exaggerate, Hawthorn.'

Hawthorn looked suitably apologetic. Martinez turned his attention to Charlotte.

'Ah, Crocodoll Dundee herself. Your airport antics have put us front page on *Variety*'s website. Nice work.'

He offered his hand and Charlotte shook it. Miss Strudworth did the introduction.

'Charlotte, this is Mr Hector Martinez, president of the movie studio.'

'He's my boss,' joked Mr Gold, 'the one who pays my bills.'

Strudworth continued, 'And this is Mr Hawthorn, vice president of the studio. Charlotte Richards, one of my best students.'

Charlotte pretty much understood the pecking order. Tommy told the actors and crew what to do, Mr Gold told Tommy what to do, Hawthorn did whatever Mr Martinez told him to do and Mr Martinez had to answer to some board about whether his movies were making any money. Mr Martinez wagged a finger at Charlotte.

'You should get your agent to talk to our TV people. They're kicking around a show, kids' *Survivor* type of thing. You'd be perfect for the host. Don't you think, Hawthorn?'

Hawthorn nodded like one of those bobbing toy dogs that the young men of Snake Hills liked to put on the dashboard of their cars.

'Absolutely.'

Much as Leila was happy for Charlotte to get attention, she drew the line when it was at her own expense. This should have been about her, not Charlie. She was contemplating a theatrical dive into the pool to win their attention when Hector Martinez turned to her.

'And here's our star!'

Got that right, Hec. Leila showed all her teeth and batted her long eyelashes. Martinez extended his arms wide to Leila, who wasted no time nuzzling his chest. She'd always liked Mr Martinez. Whenever a film wrapped he'd be sure to come to her trailer with a bag of pineapple doughnuts. And at every premiere, he always sent her a huge bouquet of flowers. Hawthorn's phone buzzed. He took the call like a frog snatching a fly and moved away from the others. Martinez turned to Joel Gold.

'So, Joel, when can I see a script?'

'Soon as I can. You know Honey Grace, she always cuts it fine.'

Hawthorn snapped his phone shut, leaned over and whispered into his boss' ear.

'Not again!' groaned Martinez. He turned to the others. 'Sorry, got a little Russell Raven problem to iron out.'

Leila chuckled to herself. Russell Raven was notorious. She wondered what he'd done this time. His last effort would have been hard to top. He was so sick of paparazzi staking out his place that he had the driveway replaced with quick-drying cement. Then he purposely had the gate left open. Those paparazzi that snuck in were all literally set in stone. Russell wouldn't allow the jackhammers in to free them for two whole days.

You had to admire a star like that. Hector Martinez and Hawthorn took their leave, with Martinez reminding Mr Gold there couldn't be any slip-ups.

'I'm serious, Joel. All our necks are out on this one.'

Joel Gold and Tommy headed up to the house to talk through some casting suggestions. Miss Strudworth announced she had some calls to make and strode off towards the bungalow where she was staying. This left Charlotte and Leila alone again.

Charlotte decided she would saddle up Leila and go for a ride around the estate.

Leila was not enthused.

'Do we have to? I mean, why don't we just kick back, have a little float in the pool, smell the smog.'

'Because in five weeks when this is over, we'll be back at Thornton Downs in competition and I don't want to have to work with a whale like last time!'

Leila was offended.

'A whale?'

'Yes, a lazy, pizza-addicted whale.' Charlotte could feel resistance but she knew how to press Leila's buttons. 'And I'm sure Warrior would agree with me.'

Hmm. Warrior . . . the kid had a point, best keep in trim. Leila trotted towards her stable.

'All right but no jumping and for every minute I exercise you have to promise to groom me two.'

'Deal,' said Charlotte. She would have stretched it to three but she wasn't letting Leila in on that.

The estate was large with tall wooded trees providing a shady grove. Charlotte realised that Mr Gold was very rich and probably capable of supplying whatever she needed to keep Leila fit.

'I might ask Mr Gold to put up some jumps while we're here.'

Jumps! Leila thought quickly to dampen the suggestion.

44

'You won't be allowed to jump me. I'm a star. They can't afford anything to happen to me.'

As Leila spoke, something rocketed out of the sky towards them, too fast for Charlotte to take evasive action. The object headed straight for Leila, veering up at the last second to clip her ear.

'Owww,' howled Leila.

The object slowed, hovered above them and spoke in a harsh, gnarled voice.

'You been here three hours and you haven't even said hello, you ungrateful starlet.'

'Hello, you feathered fathead. That what you wanted?' Leila was trying to sound angry but couldn't keep the hint of affection from her voice.

'You're Feathers!' said Charlotte, delighted to meet the bird she had heard so much about. The parrot looped the loop and landed on Charlotte's shoulder.

'In the feather, Charlotte. Nice job at the airport. By the way, I brought you a present.'

'Really?'

From under one wing Feathers dropped a small plastic gold star onto Charlotte's lap.

'For putting up with Sleeping Beauty here.'

Charlotte laughed.

'Does she still snore?' asked Feathers.

'Snore? I don't snore!' protested Leila.

Charlotte ignored her. 'You mean like this?' Charlotte did a brilliant rendition of Leila's normal snore, a high whistle that ended with a double pig grunt.

Feathers laughed loudly. 'Down to a T!'

Leila was not going to be dissed by a parrot. 'At least I can sleep, Feathers. I don't know how you can after that movie you made with Sarah-Jane set all those box-office records . . . for *least* money taken.'

Feathers' feathers ruffled. 'It was the way Tommy cut it,' he shot back.

'Hah! There's only one way he could cut it and that's around your massive beak.'

'Easier than cutting around your massive ego.'

Charlotte was lost. It was like Leila and Feathers had their own language. 'By "cut", you mean . . .?' she began to ask.

'Edit,' snapped Leila.

'Like the time they had to "edit" Leila falling at the hurdle,' quipped Feathers. 'Supposed to sail right over it and, instead, she went into a nosedive.'

'I'll edit your head from your bony shoulders,' threatened Leila.

Charlotte felt it was time to intervene. 'Now, now, you two. You know you've each missed one another. Feathers, Leila is always telling me about how you were the only decent thing in Hollywood.'

'She's exaggerating,' muttered an embarrassed Leila.

The last time Feathers had seen Leila she'd been heading off into the woods after the smell of a pizza. It had been the kidnappers' lure to trap her.

'Yeah, well, I guess things have been kind of lonely without you prancing around in front of your mirror. Nice to have you back, Princess.'

Feathers nibbled Leila's ear and she laughed.

'Hey, that tickles, cut that out.'

Charlotte enjoyed the two friends kidding around.

'So Feathers, how big is our trailer this time around?' asked Leila. 'It better be bigger than Sarah-Jane's.'

'That's the least of your worries,' said Feathers. Charlotte noted the serious tone in his voice.

'What are you talking about?' asked Leila and Charlotte simultaneously.

'I'm talking about you may not have a movie. Honey Grace just turned up in tears at Mr Gold's. She's got writer's block. Her cat went missing and now she can't write the script.'

Chapter 4

Leila insisted on heading straight over to the house to find out more. In her haste she hit near-gallop speed, bouncing Feathers off Charlotte's shoulder. Feathers decided it would be more comfortable to fly. As they neared the patio, the sound of a woman's wailing voice reached them.

'Might be best if I leave you guys,' said Feathers. 'I'd prefer Mr Gold didn't realise his prize parrot sometimes has a little outdoors time. Drop in later. I've got the Twister mat ready and raring to go.' He diverted to the top-floor window and disappeared from sight.

Charlotte could hardly believe her ears. 'Twister?'

Leila felt herself reddening. She worked so hard to project 'cool' and now that no-neck lump of sinew and feathers had blown one of her tightly held secrets.

'Feathers likes it. I feel sorry for him cooped up all day in that stuffy room.'

Charlotte smirked, 'Wait till *Entertainment Tonight* hears that Leila the wonder horse plays Twister!'

'That's enough, okay? You blab to *ET* and I'll eat your freebies to Disneyland.'

Charlotte would have laughed out loud if it hadn't been for Honey Grace's sobs. Peering through gaps in the Oscar shrubs, she was able to see a woman red-eyed and wringing her hands as tears poured from her eyes. Miss Strudworth was trying to comfort her by pouring tea. Mr Gold and Tommy Tempest had the kind of expressions on their faces that Charlotte associated with the head stockman discovering calves had been ravaged by a pack of dingoes.

'Take me through it again, Honey,' asked Mr Gold. 'You're writing the script . . .'

She was nodding vigorously, her long, dark brown hair bobbing around her face as she alternately gulped for breath and wiped away sniffles with a sodden hanky. She was dressed in a colourful long cotton skirt with calf-length leather boots and she wore big hooped earrings. Charlotte had the impression that under more normal circumstances Honey Grace would probably be quite cheerful.

She spoke as if she had gone over the story many times.

'I'm writing the script in my lounge room with the

balcony door open. Oscar doesn't come for his food. I go out to find him, he's not there . . .'

Tommy jumped in. 'So you checked the hallway?'

Honey Grace nodded and continued with difficulty. 'And then when he still didn't come for dinner I knew something was wrong. I asked everybody in the apartment block.'

Miss Strudworth cleared her throat as if she were about to raise a delicate matter.

'Sometimes cats get excited or scared and . . .' she had no choice but to utter the word, '. . . jump. Did you check the, er . . . pavement, I believe you call it here?'

'Yes. There was no sign of him. He's just . . . vanished. And it was Oscar who brought me all my good luck. I haven't been able to write a word since he disappeared. I'm so worried about him. Where could he be? Is he scared and hiding from dogs? Has somebody stolen him? I just don't know.'

The last word trailed off into a mournful howl.

'Can you believe this? Why doesn't she just get another cat?' whispered Leila.

'Because she obviously loves Oscar.'

'It's a *cat*. How can anybody love a cat? They're total users. They expect you to cater to their every whim.

They only come see you when they feel like it. They think you're beneath them . . .'

Charlotte couldn't help herself. 'Just like certain movie stars.'

Leila was indignant. 'Exactly. We movie stars have earned the right to be completely egocentric.'

'How exactly have you earned it?'

'By our emotional vulnerability. That helps us put ourselves into the characters we play. That's not just a gift, Charlie, that's hard work, all that emotion, you have to feel it in the core of your heart, you have to care for people – and here's all this fuss over a stupid missing cat!'

'Thanks for explaining that, Leila, I can really see how you care for Honey Grace in her moment of need.'

'Apology accepted.'

Charlotte shook her head. The irony was completely lost on Leila. Back on the patio, Joel Gold broached the question that had been on his mind since Honey had first arrived.

'So, Honey. How much of the script have you . . . er . . . actually written?'

'About twenty-five pages.'

Gold threw a panicked look to Tommy.

Leila gasped. 'We're sunk.'

51

'Why?'

'We begin shooting next week. Twenty-five pages will be shot in a week or two. If the cat doesn't turn up . . .'

Leila left the sentence incomplete but Charlotte understood the doom-laden expression.

'Perhaps another writer could finish it?'

Leila shook her head. 'It would be a disaster. If that cat doesn't turn up, it's no movie. And Thornton Downs –'

Leila drew a hoof across her throat. Charlotte got the picture and one glance at a worried Miss Strudworth told her she had, too. On the patio they were finishing up. Mr Gold was announcing he would buy advertising on prime time TV to get photos of Oscar flashed up. Honey Grace perked up a little as she got up to leave.

Charlotte felt very sorry for her. She whispered to Leila, 'Maybe we can help?'

'If she wants another cat, the studio can pay for it.'

'I meant *find* Oscar.'

Leila blew out through her nostrils.

'Where will I find the time? I've got rehearsals, wardrobe . . . and all-day buffets with the international press contingent.'

'I'm available.'

Honey Grace had begun moving towards her car, which was parked in the large circular driveway. Charlotte cantered Leila over.

'Excuse me, Miss Grace?'

Honey Grace looked up at the stranger, then broke into a smile.

'Leila, is that you?'

Leila batted her eyelashes and nudged Honey sympathetically. Honey hugged Leila's neck.

'Such a pretty horse. You're her groom, are you?'

Charlotte introduced herself. Honey began to apologise for her tears.

'It's perfectly understandable.' Charlotte mentioned that she knew the story of the missing cat and Honey thanked her for her concern.

'I wondered if I might be able to help you find Oscar?'

Honey seemed stunned. 'How would you do that?'

'I don't know,' admitted Charlotte truthfully. 'But back home in Snake Hills I'm pretty good at finding stray calves or tracking dingoes.'

Honey was intrigued. 'Really?'

Charlotte explained that she had little to do during the days when Leila was rehearsing.

'Haven't they given you passes for Disneyland and the studios?'

'Oh yes, Mr Gold has been very generous. But I'd rather do something useful and help find Oscar.'

'That's a very different attitude to what L.A. kids have, Charlotte. How would you get to my apartment?'

'Mr Gold has put his driver Fernando at my disposal. So, are we on?'

'Yes. Just call me and let me know when you're coming over. I'll buy some doughnuts.'

'Oh, you don't need to –'

Leila bucked hard. Charlotte got it. She was saying 'save some for me'.

'That would be nice. Bye, Miss Grace.'

'Honey, please.'

Honey Grace climbed into her car and drove off.

Leila wasted no time informing Charlotte she was crazy. 'You should hang out at the rehearsal, get a massage from the Swedish guy. Wonderful at getting the knots out.'

'If Oscar isn't found, it doesn't sound like there'll be a film. And no film means no massage.'

Leila's eyes narrowed as she thought on that. 'Hmm. Good point. Find the tabby.'

Miss Strudworth wasn't thrilled with letting Charlotte out of her sight in a big strange city like Los Angeles, but she conceded the cat needed to be found.

'Perhaps I should help too?'

They were in Leila's stables, which were almost as large as those at Thornton Downs. Leila was enjoying having her back brushed. Charlotte knew that Miss Strudworth had been looking forward to touring some equestrian centres to investigate new techniques and equipment.

'No. You need to think about Thornton Downs. And Honey Grace will be there with me. I'm sure I'll be fine.'

'Very well. But we need to make sure Mr Gold approves.'

They found him in his large den surrounded by posters showing the many films he had produced. He was pacing furiously, firing off one phone call after another. Feathers swung on a silver perch that hung from the ceiling.

'This must be the pretty Charlotte,' said Feathers in a parrot voice that sounded nothing like his true speaking voice.

'Extremely clever bird,' remarked Strudworth.

'You bet your behind, sister,' snickered Feathers.

Mr Gold got off the phone. 'I'm calling in favours

everywhere to find this cat. Even the police department is going to check the area with their choppers.'

Strudworth explained Charlotte's offer of assistance. Mr Gold shrugged.

'Charlotte, I've got professionals on this. The same guys who found where the studio hid the profits of two of my films. If they can't find Oscar, I don't think anybody can. You should be seeing Disneyland.'

'There'll be time for that when I find Oscar,' said Charlotte, with more confidence than she felt.

Mr Gold shrugged. 'Okay. Fine with me. Honey doesn't have any family here so it will probably be nice for her.'

'Charlotte will make sure she is back in time for Leila's afternoon exercise,' added Strudworth.

Mr Gold chuckled. 'Her "afternoon exercise" is usually eating pizzas and snoozing.'

'Well, not if I can help it,' added Charlotte who noticed, out of the corner of her eye, Feathers doing loop-the-loops, trying to get her attention. She had an idea what he was trying to tell her.

'I wonder if Feathers would be able to come too?'

Mr Gold looked very dubious. 'Feathers never leaves the house.'

Little did he know!

'Love to go, love to go,' said Feathers in the parrot voice.

Mr Gold relented. 'I guess it might cheer up Honey enough to start writing. Fine. But don't let the cat eat him!'

Feathers gulped. Cat? In his excitement at getting out of the house he'd completely forgotten the reason Charlotte was going. Him and his big mouth.

ↄ ↄ ↄ ↄ

Leila looked at Charlotte and Feathers with big sad eyes.

'Gee, I wish I was going with you guys.'

'No, you don't,' said Charlotte.

Leila tried to look sincere. 'How can you say that, Charlie? I, Leila, who would travel across five continents on cracked hooves . . .'

Unfortunately, at that moment the pastry cooks were wheeling a massive cake in the direction of the rehearsal building and Leila couldn't help but track it with greedy eyes.

'Ha, got you,' quipped Feathers from his gold-plated travelling cage.

One part of Leila actually did want to go with them

but today was the get-to-know-you read through where Mr Gold always laid on a spectacular buffet.

'Okay, okay, you guys know me too well. Let me put it another way. I wish you were staying here with me.'

Charlotte kissed her. 'We know that. But if Honey doesn't start writing, we're all . . .'

'. . . up the creek without a paddle,' put in Feathers.

Leila sniffed back a tear. Good old Feathers and that annoying habit he had of finishing your sentences. She'd really missed it. 'Anyways, look after yourselves.'

Leila watched them head off to the limousine where Fernando held the door open. Miss Strudworth was already inside. No point crying over spilt milkshake. It was time for business and the first priority was establishing who was the star: HER, not Sarah-Jane.

Leila looked over to where Sarah-Jane was playing tennis with her personal trainer. In addition to acting lessons from the time she was five, her lawyer mother had paid for tennis tuition. Sarah-Jane was grunting loudly as she smashed the ball back to the trainer.

Hmm. Leila recalled Mr Gold had one of those automatic tennis machines that powered balls at you. Yes, there it was on the court next to Sarah-Jane. Leila ambled casually over to the court.

'Come to watch a star . . . uggh . . . have you . . . uggh . . . Leila,' taunted Sarah-Jane, as she continued battering the ball.

It was all the incentive Leila needed. She pushed her butt against the tennis ball machine, swinging it to face Sarah-Jane, checked the feed basket was full of nice new, hard, balls and then got her teeth around the speed dial and twisted to 'maximum'. A flick of the hoof . . .

Bang!

The first ball hit Sarah-Jane in the ear.

'Ow!' she yelped, but it was drowned by the sound of balls thumping her body.

'Get that thing . . . ow . . . off you . . . ouch, idiot!' she yelled to her bodyguard, who had been standing on the other side of the court with his dark sunglasses tilted towards the sky, soaking up a few rays. She was finally forced to hit the ground and lie flat to avoid the plague of angry tennis balls. Leila watched with satisfaction as she trotted away innocently. Sometimes making movies could be fun!

ᵔ ᵔ ᵔ ᵔ

'This is where I last saw Oscar.'

Honey Grace was showing the balcony to Charlotte. Her apartment was on the first floor about eight metres above the ground. Charlotte supposed that if a cat had fallen it might still have been able to land in the soft flowerbed below, without hurting itself. The street was a quiet one with little traffic – especially for Los Angeles. The amount of traffic on the way from Mr Gold's to Honey's apartment had been unbelievable. Charlotte's mouth had been agape the whole time. She'd never seen so many cars and at one point they had all been at a total standstill. She'd wished she'd had Leila there, she could have ridden faster. She moved back a little too quickly and felt Feathers' claws dig into her shoulder.

'No quick movements, Charlie,' he whispered.

Charlotte looked over at the next balcony. It wasn't that far away.

'Could Oscar have jumped to next door's balcony?'

Honey pulled a face as she thought about it.

'Possibly but he's not a big jumper. And why would he?'

Feathers could have given a reason – 'cause all cats are psycho! Maybe he saw some poor little bird sitting on the rail there and wanted to savage it with his vicious claws!

They stepped back into the apartment, which was modestly furnished in bright colours with lots of crazy artwork on the walls.

'Let's go back to that day,' said Charlotte. 'You last remember seeing Oscar . . .'

'At about ten in the morning. Out on the balcony.'

'Then you began writing?'

'Yes.'

'And did you leave the apartment at all?'

Honey Grace thought back and became excited. 'Yes, I did. Around lunchtime. My neighbour Monica on the ground floor had cooked me a casserole, which was very kind of her.'

'Did Oscar go out with you when you went down?'

'He must have. That must have been when he got out. Oh, that naughty boy.'

Charlotte jotted all this in a small notepad.

'So you discovered him missing about three-thirty and he probably snuck out around one. That's two and a half hours.'

Honey Grace was teary. 'But I didn't raise the alarm right away. Not until six o'clock when he still hadn't shown up for his dinner.'

Charlotte asked if there was anywhere Oscar liked to investigate in the building.

'He's very friendly. He drops in on all the apartments but he's never gone out of the building before. I've searched high and low for him.'

'Maybe he's stuck somewhere?'

Charlotte had seen stories of cats stuck in the most unlikely places.

'You think? He'll be starving.'

Feathers took a look at one of the many photos around the place featuring Oscar and his doting owner. The fluffball could afford to lose some weight, probably help get itself unstuck.

Charlotte asked Honey Grace for a list of the other apartment owners. There were twelve apartments in all, which would give her quite some investigating to do. She told Honey Grace to take it easy while she did some door-knocking. When she was outside in the hall she asked Feathers what he thought.

'I think the cat wandered outside, probably after some food, and got itself lost. Cats have no sense of direction. Not like birds. I mean, you know, we have homing pigeons, we have ducks that fly thousands of miles. A cat, it could get lost in two blocks.'

'Could you ask some of your feathered pals if they saw anything?'

Feathers scratched his chin with his wing.

'I guess I could try but if this Oscar was a bird-killer don't expect any help.'

Charlotte opened the landing window and told Feathers to ask around.

'I'll meet you back here in an hour.'

'An hour? In case you haven't noticed it's kind of hard to get a watch onto my wing.'

Charlotte apologised for overlooking that. 'So how do you tell the time normally? Angle of the sun? Smells? Sounds?'

'Mostly sounds. Mr Gold leaves the radio on and the DJ gives the time.'

Serves me right, mused Charlotte. 'Okay, how about I come back here and call out to you?'

'Works for me.'

Feathers flew out the window and Charlotte began canvassing the apartments. Poor Honey Grace had been in such a state that she had not organised herself very well. She thought she had spoken to all the neighbours and asked them each to pass on to the others if they had seen anything but she couldn't be certain who she had seen and who she had not. Charlotte decided to begin at the next floor up with apartment 12 and to work her way down to the ground floor.

ↄ ↄ ↄ ↄ

'I tell you, whatever Leila has been doing, I should do. Look at her hind quarters – rock solid.'

Leila stood in the sun, soaking up the attention of the wardrobe and make-up girls.

Cassandra, the make-up girl, was the one enviously running her hand along Leila's flank. Cassandra had a liking for danish pastries, which always kept her a couple of sizes above where she wanted to be, but Leila loved her. She was forever offering Leila some of her danish, and occasionally even the odd sweet bagel.

Henrietta, the wardrobe girl, was wild with a capital Z! Leila didn't go for the jet-black hair with bright red highlights but the girl could party, and several times in the old days she'd taken Leila down to Venice Beach at sunset where they'd hung out with some really cool musician pals of hers, just strumming guitars and dancing in the sand. Leila had got right into it, dancing and swimming while Henrietta did fire-eating. Henrietta snapped a tape measure across Leila's shoulders.

'You've been working out, girl,' she said with admiration. 'Don't suppose you've read the script . . .'

If only she knew –

'. . . or what there is of it so far, but you and Sarah-Jane are going undercover to smash a wildlife-smuggling operation. The wardrobe I have in mind is going to be a fantastic colour palette. You'll be going to Mexico . . .'

Really? Leila could taste the tamales already.

'. . . I'm going to put you in this!' With a flourish, Henrietta produced a sombrero studded with . . . Were they diamonds?

'Of course these aren't real diamonds, they're zircon.'

Leila's face fell. She was a star, she deserved diamonds.

Henrietta continued, 'But it's still real pretty, no, amigo?'

Leila conceded it did have a certain something. Henrietta produced a sketchpad.

'I'll also be putting you in this poncho. Now, I know what you're thinking, Leila . . .'

Poncho! PONCHO!!! For a glamour girl like me?

'. . . you're thinking a poncho is downbeat.'

Darn right she was thinking that. That horrible coarse wool itched like . . . well, horse blankets.

'. . . but you only wear the poncho while undercover. Later, when you are on the ranch of the kingpin wildlife-smuggler as Sarah-Jane gets information, you'll be in this – a pure silk poncho.'

Henrietta produced another sketch and some fabric that she rubbed against Leila's flank. It was divine.

'When you go to Tokyo on the trail, it will be a kimono . . .'

Wait a minute, did she say Tokyo? Like all stars Leila only ever read the script pages where her dialogue was mentioned. Tokyo, wow! Leila had always wanted to ride the bullet train.

'Of course you won't actually be going to Mexico or San Diego, that will all be shot in the hills. And Tokyo will be downtown L.A.'

Leila's excitement sank. She had forgotten for a moment that the movie industry was all about fooling people into thinking something was real. It was the first time she'd thought of Charlotte and Feathers since they'd gone this morning. Now those guys were real. She wished she was with them instead of this, fake, false . . . Oh-oh, what was that Cassandra had just produced from her bag?

'Here, Leila, like a little danish?'

On second thoughts, she'd be catching up with them later. Right now, Leila was needed here with the danish.

ɔ ɔ ɔ ɔ

It took Charlotte almost the whole hour to cover the other eleven apartments, even though nobody was home in four of them. There was a wide variety of tenants, that was for sure, and not one of them was anything like her dad and the people of Snake Hills. Honey's friend Monica, though, did bear a physical resemblance to Mrs Cuthbert, who worked in the pie shop. That was about the extent of their similarity. Monica informed Charlotte she was a vegetarian, which, of course, would be the last person you'd find working in a pie shop. When she learned Charlotte's father was a stockman she looked very grave. Stockmen rounded up cattle who wound up being slaughtered and served on dinner plates and between sandwich buns, she said. She told Charlotte he should look for some other occupation. Charlotte had explained that in Snake Hills there was no other occupation. Apart from that hiccup Monica was friendly. She gave Charlotte some real lemonade and happily answered all the questions about the day Oscar disappeared. She did not remember him coming down with Honey, nor had she seen him on the stairs. She had never known him to stray, though he occasionally sunned himself in the garden. Monica suspected that apartment 4 might be the culprit.

'She's an idiot. The noise! And I've caught her peeing in the hallway.'

Charlotte was not looking forward to meeting this woman.

'What's her name?'

'Buffy. That shocking flat face with no nose. I hate Pekinese.'

'Buffy's a dog?'

'Yes. Although personally I think Pekinese should be classified differently.'

Buffy's owner was a man named Nigel. Tall and slim with a moustache. He was actually very friendly although he kept darting in and out to check on some ceramic vase he was selling on eBay. Nigel had not seen Oscar at all that day. He stroked Buffy, who looked accusingly at Charlotte when she asked if Buffy might have chased Oscar.

'Buffy likes Oscar. Besides, she was at the vet that day having a procedure.'

None of the other tenants were much use. They were all actors or actresses who had evening jobs. Some of them didn't even know Oscar. All of them were either in bed or watching TV at the time Oscar disappeared. One of them, a skinny girl with a stud in her nose, recalled a window cleaner that day.

'He might have seen something.'

'Do you know where to find him?'

She thought about it.

'His van was parked out there when I went to get a slurpy but I don't remember if there was a name on the side of it.'

Charlotte re-canvassed all the apartments. One of the men on the top floor, who continued to work on his rowing machine as Charlotte questioned him, now recalled seeing the window cleaner doing first-floor windows but didn't know who he'd been working for. Monica suspected he was probably working for the Grants.

'Who are they?'

'They are in the apartment next to Honey but they're on vacation at the moment in Canada. They're always having people in doing cable TV or air-conditioning or something.'

'How long have they been away?'

Monica wasn't sure but thought it was a day or two before Oscar had gone missing.

'I don't have their phone number but Honey probably will.'

Feeling that she'd at least achieved something, Charlotte went down into the laundry on the basement level and checked around in case Oscar had gone investigating down there. She looked behind all the machines but found nothing. The hour was almost up. She went outside and checked the garden. No sign of Oscar but she did find some indentations that probably came from the legs of a ladder. The window cleaner, no doubt.

'Any luck?'

The deep voice scared her until she realised it was Feathers.

'I was up on the satellite dish catching some rays,' he explained.

Charlotte gave a run-down of what she had learned. 'How about you?'

'I learned quite a lot. Like a whole heap of people leave out seed for the cousins to feed. Totally free. And you know the parks people actually try to poison those poor pigeons? Granted, pigeons leave a little to be desired hygiene-wise . . .'

Charlotte was forced to cut in.

'I meant about Oscar.'

'Oh, the tabby! Yeah. Let me think.'

Feathers angled his head as he searched through his brain. 'You know, Charlie, next time we should do it in fifteen-minute lots. I got nothing to write with and it's hard to remember everything.'

Charlotte tried to be patient.

'Sorry, Feathers, I'll keep that in mind. Did any of the birds see Oscar that day?'

'Firstly, they said Oscar is a sweetheart. Never chases them. But there is a wild cat around who is like carnage on four paws. Apparently he and Oscar got into a scrap once in the flowerbed.'

Charlotte noted that. Maybe the stray cat had chased Oscar?

'Then there's some ugly dog lives in there.'

'Buffy.'

'Whatever. It chases Oscar but Oscar isn't scared of it and has clawed it back. That was about all I got of any use. Except there is a wonderful birdbath two blocks over – marble, with a little waterfall.'

Charlotte listened to Feathers rave about the birdbath and then came back to the main question.

'But none of them have seen Oscar out in the streets?'

'No sir.'

Charlotte wasn't sure if that was a good or bad thing. They returned to Honey's place and Charlotte brought her up to speed. Honey was excited about the window cleaner and called the Grants' mobile phone to get the name. Unfortunately they didn't answer so she had to leave a message.

'They may not have even taken their phone with them,' she said, her anxiety climbing again. As for the stray cat and Buffy, she had no idea.

'Perhaps they chased Oscar?' she said, echoing Charlotte's thoughts.

'He hasn't been seen in the streets,' said Charlotte.

'You canvassed the streets as well?'

Charlotte sidestepped. 'I asked some people with a bird's-eye view.'

Honey Grace sighed. 'You've been really wonderful, Charlotte. Let me make you a hot chocolate before the car comes to get you.'

Charlotte didn't need a hot chocolate. 'There's something else I should check out.'

Honey was all ears.

'The Grants' apartment. What if Oscar jumped over there and the window cleaner locked him in accidentally?'

Honey's face registered the possibility. 'Oh my goodness.'

Charlotte could see Honey's mounting anxiety.

'But I don't have a key and they're away.'

Charlotte said she was pretty sure she could at least get a good look through their balcony doors. Honey Grace was perplexed. 'But how would you get to their balcony?'

'The usual way. Jump.'

'No, it's too dangerous. I'll get a ladder.'

'Do you have one?'

She didn't. She would have to buy one and she wasn't sure if the local store would be open. But there was a Costco about thirty minutes away. Charlotte calculated that they would run out of time.

'It's okay, I've done this before.'

This was a slight exaggeration. She had once found herself clinging to the windowsill of Todd's room high above the grounds at Milthorp but hadn't actually had to jump, and she had once had to jump from her window at Thornton Downs to a tree branch, but never balcony to balcony.

Feathers whispered, 'This is crazy, kid. Let me take a look.'

Charlotte saw the sense in that.

'I'm going to send Feathers over. If there's a cat inside he'll come rushing straight back. Actually, I'm very thirsty. Honey, could you get me another lemonade?'

'Of course.'

Honey took herself inside, allowing Charlotte time to brief Feathers.

'Get a look through the verandah and then across to the bedroom window.'

'Aye, aye, cap'n.' Feathers put on a pirate voice. Charlotte rolled her eyes. Feathers became defensive. 'Hey, it's Hollywood, everybody has a little schtick.'

Just as Feathers was about to take off, a large black bird circled above.

'Oh-oh, bandit at twelve o'clock,' said Feathers, and Charlotte noted his scaly legs shaking.

'What's up?'

'That's a raven. They don't like us parrots.'

The bird continued to circle threateningly. Charlotte couldn't allow Feathers to be attacked.

'You take yourself inside. I've got this.'

Feathers didn't need any more encouragement. He was inside in a flash. Charlotte scaled the rail of the balcony. It wasn't that far, she told herself. Only a couple of metres across . . . and a very long way down.

Chapter 5

One of the great delights of doing a movie was the pedicure. Consuela was a marvel. Okay, Charlotte was no slouch with a hoof-pick but Consuela had magic hands. As she worked that magic, Leila closed her eyes and drifted. Tommy Tempest was droning on to Sarah-Jane about her character's motivation in wanting to bust the wildlife racket. The actor who played her mother was having her hands moisturised and somebody in the crew was snoring. It was the same every time, everything on hold for the brat. Poor Tommy, it wasn't his fault. Ah, Consuela, the way you file!

'. . . see, you don't like animals being smuggled so you want to bust the racket.'

'Hmm,' said Sarah-Jane doubtfully. 'Why don't I like animals being smuggled?'

'Because it's wrong,' Tommy choked in frustration.

'But if people are paying big money for these

animals they are going to be well looked after,' countered Sarah-Jane.

'Yes but a cheetah wants to run in the wild, not in a five-star hotel.'

'Have you spoken to one?'

Leila hated to admit it but the kid had a point. Life in a five-star hotel wasn't exactly ball-and-chain stuff. So far four hours and they were still on page one. Leila lifted her other hoof for Consuela.

Tommy's grip on his crutches was growing weak.

'Okay, Sarah-Jane, why do you think you might be motivated to smash the wildlife-smuggling ring?'

Obviously Sarah-Jane had been waiting for the invitation for the last four hours and had her answer all planned out.

'How about I will receive a gold medal from the World Wildlife people for risking my life for the animals?'

Tommy nodded.

'Terrific, we'll work that in. A gold medal is much better than you actually caring for the animals.'

He infused it with as much sarcasm as he could but it sailed over Sarah-Jane's head and she simply smiled smugly that she had made her point. Tommy ran his fingers through his hair. 'We'll take a coffee break.'

The actors and crew quickly got up and dispersed.

Much to Leila's disappointment, even Consuela. One of the crew members held back. Leila knew this was Mac who operated the boom. He looked around as if to make sure nobody was watching, took out his mobile phone and dialled.

'Freddy, it's Mac. Look, about the money I owe . . . I'll get it, okay? But I need you to stake me one more bet . . .'

Oh dear, a gambler and obviously in hock to some bookmaker.

'Come on, please, Freddy, just let me have fifty on the nose, number six, race three, Del Mar.'

On the nose. Leila hated the way they used that expression about horses. She found it on the nose, in fact.

Mac was feverish. 'Collateral? My van, okay? But look, I've got a payout coming in from something else. Thanks.'

This idiot was thanking the bookmaker for allowing him to take his money? Go figure humans. They did the craziest things.

ɔ ɔ ɔ ɔ

Charlotte stood on the balcony rail feeling the breeze much stronger away from the protection of the walls.

She took a deep breath, summoned her strength and jumped . . .

Everything seemed to slow as she glided across towards the Grants' balcony. It seemed oh so easy . . . and then all of a sudden she began to plummet and time raced forward. One moment she was almost there, the next the balcony was rushing past. She threw out a hand, felt the iron railing and a jolt on her shoulder. For a horrible moment she was cycling in thin air and then she hauled herself up and onto the balcony.

She let out a long sigh. Close call.

She stepped across towards the wide glass door and tried to peer in. The sunlight reflecting off the dust made it a little hard to see in. Curtains restricted vision into the apartment but there was a five-centimetre gap between the two edges in the middle. Charlotte pressed her face right up against the glass and could see most of the lounge room.

'Oscar?' she called but there was no sudden appearance of a tabby.

Honey Grace came out onto her balcony holding the lemonade, and exclaimed in shock, 'Charlotte!'

'It's okay. No sign of him in the lounge.'

She looked over to where the bedroom window was another couple of metres beyond the balcony's edge. This would be easy for Feathers. She glanced skywards. The threatening raven hadn't left. Oh, well. She climbed up onto the rail. A drainpipe was about a metre away.

'No, Charlotte . . .' cried Honey, from somewhere behind her. Charlotte put it out of her head and stretched over. She was able to grip the pipe. It seemed stable. She hooked her right leg around it and let go of the railing. Now she was gripping the pipe like a koala up a gum tree. She hauled herself up and peered in the bedroom. Her heat leapt, there on the chair . . . a ball of fur!

But just as quickly her heart sank. It was only a fur hat. She was able to scan the whole bedroom though. No sign of Oscar. What a disappointment!

ᔓ ᔓ ᔓ ᔓ

What a disappointment! Consuela had packed up her kit for the day and, by the looks of it, everybody else was readying to leave as Tommy held forth.

'We'll reconvene tomorrow and read the rest of the script. We start shooting Thursday.'

'That's the day after tomorrow!' bellowed Sarah-Jane. 'Tommy, how can you expect me to be up to speed with one read through? We haven't even seen the full script.'

'You've seen everything there is to see.'

'What's Honey Grace doing for goodness sake? *Writers.*' Sarah-Jane shook her head bitterly.

'Granted it's not the optimum situation but that's the way it is. We have to start shooting with what we have.'

'Today has been a total waste.' Sarah-Jane folded her arms and looked accusingly at Tommy, who had dealt with enough of her tantrums not to be riled.

'Not a total waste, Sarah-Jane. You gave us that great bit about the gold medal from the World Wildlife Fund, remember?'

Tommy broke off before Sarah-Jane could complain further. Leila felt her stomach begin to knot. In forty-eight hours they would begin shooting. Would she be up to it? It had been over a year since she'd smelt her skin sweating under the hot lights of a shoot. Under Consuela's magic her anxiety had temporarily gone but now it was all coming back.

'Gee, Leila, you got knots in you like an oak tree, darlink,' said Consuela in her thick accent as she patted her goodbye. She wasn't whistling Dixie. Being a star was scary. Leila relaxed slightly when she saw the limousine pull into the roundabout. Her pals were back. Unfortunately they couldn't stand beside her in front of the camera. She saw Mac, the boom guy, take a text on his phone and then throw it away in anger. Guess the nag he'd backed lost. Leila could have had a word to the horses for him had she known, but most of the time they had no idea themselves if they would win. Maybe Charlie pulled something off at Honey's after all? Leila cantered over to find out.

ᴖ ᴖ ᴖ ᴖ

'So you got nothing, nada, zilch,' said Leila as they trotted around the property later.

'I wouldn't say nothing,' snapped Feathers. 'I found this birdbath, marble with a little waterfall . . .'

Charlotte cut in, 'Like I told you. I got the lead on the window cleaner. If the Grants get back to Honey then I can follow that up. He was there around the right time and might have seen something.'

Leila shuffled restlessly. 'This was all a stupid idea.'

Charlotte detected the change in tone. 'What's up?'

Leila sighed. 'What if I'm no good? What if I forget where I'm supposed to be standing or rear up when I'm supposed to lie down? What if the cinematographer shoots my bad profile?'

'You know what you need?'

'Yes, but you can't get it without a prescription.'

'You don't need pills, Leila, you need a good run.'

Feathers chirped in that there was a marvellous riding trail through the Hollywood Hills. He pointed his wing in the direction.

'Mr Gold will never let me out. I'm too valuable,' sighed Leila.

'Then let's not tell Mr Gold,' said Charlotte.

Feathers shuddered. 'Not tell Mr Gold? Are you serious?'

'He's got a lot on his mind anyway,' said Charlotte. 'Can you direct us?'

'Me? It'll be dark in an hour and there're coyotes in those hills.'

Leila shifted uneasily. 'Bird brain has a point.'

Charlotte dismissed it. 'If I can deal with a pack of dingoes I can deal with a coyote.'

'Maybe *you* can but what about us?' Feathers was shaking all over.

'All right, Feathers, you go back to your cage but, Leila, no excuses. You're coming for a good gallop.'

'You can't get out except through the security gate,' said Feathers.

'Nonsense. Those walls don't look too high.'

'Jump? I don't know about jumping . . .' began Leila but it was too late. Charlotte was already driving her boot heels into Leila's flank.

'Come on, chicken-heart,' she yelled.

Chicken-heart! Nobody called Leila chicken-heart. She set herself towards the outdoor furniture and leapt high over the cluster of umbrellas, clearing the wall easily.

Charlie was right. It was exhilarating . . .

. . . except on the way down, on the neighbours' side, Leila saw a garden of cacti. Oh no!

She stretched as if she was reaching for the last slice of four-cheeses pizza and cleared the cacti spines by a fraction. A bunch of people were out in the garden having a barbecue. Leila knew Mr Gold's neighbour wasn't anybody famous, just a very good dentist, and she could see his handiwork as the people stared open-mouthed at Charlie galloping past on Leila.

'G'day,' waved Charlotte to the stunned group.

'That's . . . that's Leila,' shrieked a little girl ecstatically. By the time she had finished the sentence they had crossed the lawn and jumped the next fence.

Using their backyard shortcuts it took them not much more than half an hour to get to the Hollywood Hills. It was incredible to think that so close to the world's busiest freeways could be such vast, natural scrubland. Leila enjoyed playing tour guide.

'You know the movie industry was based in New York to start with but they moved it out here because they could shoot longer in the natural light. A lot of L.A. was orange groves.'

Charlotte found that hard to believe.

'And all up around here they used for the early westerns. We've shot up here a couple of times. In fact we started the second movie shooting the last scene where I free Sarah-Jane from being trapped in a mine shaft, right here.'

That didn't sound right to Charlotte.

'You mean the first scene, don't you?'

Leila giggled. 'You know nothing about movies, do you? You don't shoot scene one first and scene two next and so on.'

'You don't?'

'No, you'd spend your whole day moving around. You shoot all the scenes in that location, then move onto the next location and do all the scenes set there. Then you cut and paste them together to make the film.'

Now Charlotte finally understood what Leila and Feathers meant by 'cut'.

Leila was on a roll. 'People think acting is easy but see, you might have to play out how you're feeling at the end of the film and then, an hour later, play out how you're feeling at the beginning of the film, before anything has happened to you.'

Charlotte conceded that was quite a skill. She felt at home in these hills in the quiet. It was so pretty now. The breeze made the low scrub ripple like little waves.

'The smog doesn't seem so bad up here,' observed Charlotte. If she didn't look at the sprawling city in the distance at the foot of the hills she could almost think herself back home in Snake Hills.

Leila herself was feeling better already.

'I gotta say, Charlie, this was a good call. I'm loosening up. Say, why don't we drop into the Whiskey on the way back?'

'That's what, some club?'

Leila snorted, 'The Whiskey isn't "some club", it's a historical landmark. Even better the studio runs a tab there, which means we don't have to pay for drinks.'

Charlotte reminded Leila she wasn't old enough to go into a club like that.

'It's Hollywood. Just say you've recently been to Palm Springs for a facelift.'

'No. That would be lying.'

'Lying in Hollywood isn't wrong, it's part of the place. Just like food is in Paris or snow is in Moscow.'

'I don't care. I'm not going to lie to get into some club.'

'Such a goody two shoes,' muttered Leila. Then a thought occurred. 'Maybe you could wait outside . . .'

'Forget it.'

Leila sulked. They walked in silence for a while. Charlotte announced something was bugging her about the visit to Honey's but she couldn't put her finger on it.

'Did Honey order in some pizza for you?'

'No.'

'There you go.'

'That's not it. It's something about Oscar going missing. It's right in front of my face . . .'

Right in front of her face . . . even that phrase was important. What was it?

Leila slowed to a crawl.

'Er, Charlotte, I think you should worry about that later.'

Charlotte was annoyed. 'Why not worry about it now?'

'Because right now I'd rather you worry about that coyote in front of us.'

Charlotte had been gazing at the sunset. Now she swung her gaze to the path and, sure enough, there was a large, lean animal standing right there, mouth part open, panting. Leila made to run but Charlotte reefed her back.

'What do you think you're doing?'

'Showing that coyote the designer horseshoes on my rear hooves. *What do you think I'm doing*?' Leila was growing hysterical.

Charlotte had never seen a coyote but she knew the difference between a cat and a dog.

'I don't think that's a coyote.'

'You think it's a rock formation that looks like a coyote?' Leila squinted, a hopeful lilt to her voice.

'No, I think it's a mountain lion.'

Leila began trembling. She looked at the long muscular body, the whiskers. She could imagine razor sharp teeth sinking into her gorgeous legs.

'O-kay,' said Leila in a high sing-song voice as she began edging backwards. Charlotte stopped her again.

'No. It might be part of a family. In which case, they will have come around behind us.'

'*We're trapped?*' Leila was freaking. 'I'm going to be torn apart by a pack of mountain lions and I've never even had the Oscar I deserve. Why me? God, why me? Why not Sarah-Jane?'

'Quiet, Leila.'

The mountain lion or large bobcat or whatever it was swished its tail and took a slow step forward.

'What are we going to do?'

'What do you think? You weigh five times what it does. Would you walk in front of a speeding bus?'

Leila thought about it. 'Maybe if there was some pepperoni . . .'

'Yaghhh!' Charlotte yelled and dug her heels into Leila, who shot forward reflexively.

'*Are you mad?*' she screamed as she thundered towards the startled mountain lion, who had clearly not anticipated this response.

Charlotte could see the mountain lion considering whether to attack but deciding at the last moment the horse was too crazy. It sprang to the side as Charlotte and Leila thundered by. Leila didn't stop until they were all the way down the bottom of the canyon.

For the return trip Leila refused to go via the Hollywood Hills. Instead they padded around back streets. The air was warm and the ride back to Joel Gold's was pleasant. They cut up a side street and jumped across backyards, returning with a thump to the dark reaches of Mr Gold's estate. They had only just emerged from the thick foliage when Strudworth came towards them.

'I've been looking for you, Charlotte.'

'Any news?'

'Yes. There's been a fabulous response to the TV ads about Oscar. It sounds like he's been found only a few blocks away from the apartment. Honey Grace is going over to get him.'

Charlotte was so relieved. 'Thank goodness for that.'

Strudworth ticked the air with a finger as something else occurred. 'Oh, and Todd Greycroft called from San Diego. They had their first day of competition today. He's going to call back tomorrow. What have you been doing?'

Charlotte caught Leila looking up at her. 'Oh, nothing much, just a little exercise.'

When Strudworth had turned back Leila had great pleasure in needling Charlie.

'Told you. When you're in Hollywood, it's perfectly acceptable to lie. Now, what do you think they'll have for supper tonight?'

ɔ ɔ ɔ ɔ

Charlotte was disappointed to have missed Todd's call but that was outweighed by the good news about Oscar being found. Now she wouldn't have to try to remember whatever it was that had been bugging her before about Oscar's disappearance. She sat next to Miss Strudworth at the very long dinner table in Mr Gold's dining room and heard all about what Miss Strudworth had accomplished during her excursion. It was mainly to do with training techniques and Charlotte didn't understand it too well, especially with her head fuzzy and eyes beginning to droop. It was a much happier Mr Gold, too. He thanked Charlotte again for taking the time to help Honey Grace.

'Not that I did any good,' said Charlotte.

'That's not true, Charlotte. Honey told me it was very comforting to have somebody she didn't even know caring so much. Now perhaps we should see if your bedroom has arrived.'

Charlotte thought she may have misheard.

'Come with me,' said Mr Gold, and Charlotte followed him down a very long corridor adorned with photos of Mr Gold with various movie stars. Mr Gold pointed to a series of close-ups. In each one he was framed beside a different man in a suit. 'All presidents,' he said.

Charlotte gasped. There were at least nine.

'How often do you have elections here?'

Mr Gold chuckled.

'Not presidents of the U.S., Charlotte, much more important – presidents of the studio. And no elections, they just get fired every couple of years.'

Charlotte stopped at a photo of Mr Gold looking out of place on a basketball court.

'But that one . . .'

'Oh yes, that one *is* the President of the United States.'

They emerged into a very large back courtyard. A prime mover was just leaving, the driver waving to Fernando. It had deposited the largest caravan Charlotte had ever seen.

'This is where you and Leila stay.'

Charlotte's jaw dropped. Mr Gold smiled.

'It's the biggest in the country. Nothing's too good for my star. You want to go get her?' Mr Gold told Charlotte if there was anything she needed, just call on the phone in the trailer.

'They've put in a line for you. Button 1 goes to the kitchen. If you're hungry, just tell them what you want; button 2 is for Fernando if you need to be driven anywhere; button 3 is Sven the masseur and button 4 will get you housekeeping. Anything else, find me.' He excused himself to return to Miss Strudworth.

Charlotte found Leila in the stables enjoying a large bucket of pesto pasta.

'Mr Gold's cook Nunzio really has the touch. What did you guys eat?'

Charlotte laughed, Leila's mouth was a deep green from the pesto. 'We had fish.'

'Canadian trout with a white wine sauce? Nunzio does that very nicely.'

'Our accommodation has arrived.'

Leila stopped eating immediately. 'Then what are we waiting for? I mean, the barn is all right in a "quaint, rustic" way but there's no cable and no wide-screen plasma.'

Leila began trotting out of there so fast Charlotte had to mount her. As they rounded the corner into the rear courtyard, Leila began drooling.

'Oh yes. Oh yes, yes. I like it.'

Charlotte dismounted and walked Leila up the ramp into the enormous trailer. She had never seen anything like it. Leila's 'stall' was quilted and the 'straw' was some kind of soft synthetic sponge.

'This stuff is great. No itch and no annoying hay fever. But has he done my air-conditioning how I like?' She looked down and smiled at a plastic hoof-shaped pedal. 'Hoof control. I can adjust the temperature higher or lower.' She walked on a little further and sighed in ecstasy.

'That's what I call a plasma.'

The screen took up almost half of one entire wall. It must have been three metres long. It was followed immediately by a mirror the same size.

'Girl has to look her best,' sniggered Leila, who already had a little spring to her step. Opposite the mirror was a running machine, although this was closer to the size of the travelators in the airport.

'At least you can exercise,' observed Charlotte.

'No way! Sarah-Jane has one so I just threw a tantrum until they worked out I wanted one as well. Look at the pizza oven!'

Sure enough, there was a full-size pizza oven in the kitchen area.

'I thought I just called the kitchen on the phone?'

'That's while we're here but when we go on set, my chef comes in and cooks for us.'

Charlotte's bed was at the other end of the trailer. It was larger than the one she had at Thornton Downs.

'So, how about we microwave a little popcorn and take in a movie?' Leila was already nudging the remote with her nose, changing the channels on the plasma.

Charlotte flicked it off. 'No. I'm tired and you have to get a good night's rest. It's rehearsal tomorrow.'

'Party-pooper,' grumbled Leila as she slunk back to her stall. Charlotte knew Leila must have been tired herself or she would have argued longer.

Charlotte's bag had been delivered to the trailer. She put on her pyjamas and climbed into bed. 'Good night, Leila.'

'Night, Charlie.'

Charlotte switched off the light. The longest day of her life swam through her head, all the things that had happened tumbling over one another. She was vaguely aware of Leila snoring but was too tired to care. She let go of the world and sleep took her.

Chapter 6

Leila was floating on a large air bed in the biggest pool you could ever imagine. Warrior swam behind her, pushing.

'A little to the left, the sun is in my eyes.'

'Get up, fathead.'

What had happened to Warrior's voice? Gone was that deep tone as rich and smooth as chocolate. Now it seemed scratchy and annoying . . .

'Come on, fathead, move it.'

Ouch. Something was nibbling her . . . SHARKS!

Leila shook her head. The air bed deflated, the pool shrank. She was in the trailer . . . and Feathers was nibbling her ear.

'Thanks a lot, Feathers, I was having the best dream.'

She looked over. Charlie was fast asleep.

'Ver-ry nice,' said Feathers, checking out the interior of the trailer.

'You hungry?' asked Leila.

'I could eat a horse.'

'Ha ha. Muesli?'

'You got it.'

Leila clicked the phone line to the kitchen.

'Yes?' asked one of the helpers.

Leila put on an Australian accent to sound like Charlotte.

'Could I have two bacon and eggs on rye, lightly toasted, eggs sunnyside, bacon crispy. And a muesli, please?'

'Of course,' came the woman's voice. 'Any juice?'

'What have you got?'

'Cranberry, tomato, lemon, grapefruit, celery, carrot, apple, orange, pear, grape . . .'

'Give us a couple of pear and apple with a twist of lemon. Thank you.' Leila hung up and sighed. 'Bring back memories?'

Feathers nodded at the thought of shared past adventures. 'You guys have fun last night?'

Leila told the story of the mountain lion, with an embellishment or two.

'So the kid is screaming, "get me out of here". I say, Charlie, these are lions, they hunt in packs. They're probably waiting behind us right now . . .'

'That's not how I remember it,' came Charlotte's sleepy voice, behind them.

'Kid, you were overwrought from the travel. Your mind is playing tricks.'

Charlotte said her mind wasn't capable of that many tricks. She gave her account as she got ready to shower.

'I know who I believe,' said Feathers.

Leila pointed her nose at Charlotte. 'See. Feathers knows me.'

'I meant *her*!' said Feathers.

Before Leila could object there was a knock on the caravan door.

'Charlotte, are you up yet?' It was Strudworth.

'Just a minute.' Charlotte went over and opened the door to find a distressed Miss Strudworth.

'Bad news, I'm afraid . . .'

Before she could give the bad news a young woman arrived with the breakfast order.

'Oh, bacon and eggs, how thoughtful you ordered for me, Charlotte.'

Leila watched in horror as Strudworth began to tuck into *her* bacon and eggs.

'Sorry, but I eat when I'm worried,' she explained. She wasn't joking! She moved quickly on to the muesli. Feathers watched aghast. Charlotte flicked some bacon Leila's way while Strudworth's head was down.

'What's the bad news?' asked Charlotte, noting Feathers and Leila fighting over the bacon rasher.

'The cat. It wasn't Oscar. We're back to square one.'

At the rehearsal area actors and crew were drifting in, scripts in hand while the kitchen staff frantically tried to get breakfast ready, polishing cutlery and setting it out on the enormous L-shaped trestle table with massive bowls of cut fruit, plates of pastries and pots of coffee. Honey Grace was pacing, gulping a mug of steaming coffee, looking like she was contemplating death by firing squad. Her sad eyes latched onto Charlotte.

'Oh, Charlotte! You heard the news?'

Charlotte explained she had.

'I was so happy last night when I thought he had been found. The cat looked a little bit like him but it wasn't my Oscar. I don't know what to do. I couldn't sleep. I know I should be writing but I can't. I just can't think. And everybody is relying on me, and I'm letting them down and –' she ran out of steam – 'it's just awful.'

Charlotte didn't know what comfort she could offer but she tried her best. 'If Oscar is out there, alive somewhere, he needs you to keep calm.'

Honey nodded vigorously. 'You're right. I have to think of Oscar.'

'Have the Grants called back?'

Honey had to think for a moment. 'About the window cleaner? No, they haven't. Maybe I should try them again.'

Charlotte looked for Leila, who had been right behind her on the way from the trailer. She now saw her hanging around the pastries. Typical. As the kitchenhand brought out yet more gleaming cutlery, something suddenly clicked into place for Charlotte and she knew what had been bugging her yesterday.

'They weren't clean,' she exclaimed.

'What weren't?'

Charlotte beamed, certain in her knowledge. 'The windows of the Grants' apartment. When I went to look inside it was almost impossible because of the dust. I had to wipe it away and press my eyes to the glass.'

Honey shook her head sadly.

'Unfortunately, nowadays you can't rely on any-body. I suppose he knew they were away and just did a slap-dash job.'

'Or he didn't do a job at all.'

'But people saw him.'

Charlotte corrected Honey. 'People saw somebody up a ladder with a cap and overalls. Somebody who looked like a window cleaner.'

Honey was lost. 'But who else would be up a ladder looking like a window cleaner?'

ᔓ ᔓ ᔓ ᔓ

'A thief?'

Miss Strudworth sounded doubtful. She and Charlotte were standing in Mr Gold's enormous living room, which was painted with a mural of Leila and Sarah-Jane from *Horses for Courses*, a movie in which Leila had enrolled at university for a term. Leila had been left with Consuela while the script read-through continued.

'I'm sure there are people who steal cats but it seems an awful lot of trouble to go to. What did Honey Grace think?'

'Much the same,' said Charlotte, feeling a little downcast. 'The people in the apartment block didn't need a ladder to steal Oscar and nobody else really knew him.'

'Well, if this window cleaner's credentials don't check out, your theory will have credibility, but I still can't see why they wanted the cat.'

'Maybe there is somebody out there who dislikes Honey for some reason and wants to hurt her.'

'Hmm.' Strudworth thought on this. 'Charlotte, that is very astute. Did you ask her?'

Charlotte had not mentioned it to Honey for fear of upsetting her. Strudworth was nodding slowly, pacing, turning over the possibilities.

'A jilted boyfriend perhaps? Some men do that kind of thing, Charlotte, which is why I only ever allowed Zucchini into my life. Or, professional jealousy. Let's face it, this is a ruthless town. Perhaps some other writer who was overlooked . . .'

Just then one of Mr Gold's assistants appeared. She was expensively dressed and, as on every other occasion Charlotte had spied her, carried some electronic device in her hand.

'Excuse me. Is one of you Charlotte Richards?'

Charlotte put up her hand.

'There's a phone call for you. A Mr Todd Greycroft. If you'd like to follow me?'

Charlotte turned back to Strudworth, who reassured her.

'I'll ask Mr Gold about Honey's enemies. He might have some idea. And tell Todd to make sure he goes hard on the first round and puts the pressure on the other riders.'

Mr Gold's assistant – 'I'm Zara by the way' – indicated a room off to the right. It was very neat and looked hardly used. The wooden table on which the phone sat was brightly polished with a deep red-brown hue. Charlotte sat in one of the brocade chairs and felt like some princess back in the days of horses, carriages and candlelight.

'Hi, Todd.'

'Hey, Charlie, how's it going there?' Todd sounded bright and bubbly as usual.

Charlotte didn't mean to, but with the chance to finally converse with somebody her own age and mindset she spilled out all the trials and tribulations of the last twenty-four hours. Explaining the missing Oscar, the extraordinary trailer and the encounter with the mountain lion took a good ten minutes.

'Wow,' said Todd when she finished. 'My time can't compare to that.'

Charlotte felt guilty. She hadn't even enquired about his eventing. 'So how have you gone so far?'

Todd gave a run-down of the competition, which involved riders from all over the world.

'The Argentinians are very good and the Germans almost as good as you at dressage.'

Todd had scored top points of the Milthorp contingent but was only in eleventh place overall after the dressage. Charlotte thought that was encouraging because it was jumping and cross-country where Todd really excelled.

'Hope you're right.'

Todd announced that he had to go and get ready for the jumps. 'I'll see you in Los Angeles next week,' he said.

'If Oscar doesn't turn up we may not be here next week.'

'You'll come up with something, Charlie,' he said before ringing off.

Charlotte wished she could believe that. She really did.

ↄ ↄ ↄ

They had got through the first read and were taking a break before they tried moving a couple of the action scenes. Leila walked around the perimeter, soaking up the sun and snooping. She particularly enjoyed the look on Sarah-Jane's face when she clapped eyes on Leila's trailer. Pure envy. Sarah-Jane snapped out her pearl-tinted mobile and immediately called her agent.

'Herb, it's me . . . How am I? I'll tell you how I am, Herb. Very, very unhappy. I'm standing here being forced to look at a trailer at least four feet longer than mine . . . So what if Leila's a horse? She's got you all fooled. I want my trailer to be just as big.' Her face went into spasm. 'What do you mean the only one in the country?'

Suck it up, baby. Leila was lapping it up. All she needed now to top it off was a fat danish. She left Sarah-Jane ranting to her agent and was trotting past the crew gathered around the coffee urn when she spied a barely touched pastry left on a crate. Finders keepers. As she neared the pastry she saw Mac, the sound guy, on his phone again. Probably trying to gamble away more of his money. Mac looked around furtively in case anybody was eavesdropping, but paid no attention to Leila as she edged closer and snaffled the pastry.

'I told you, Freddy, I transferred the money to your account. Check it . . .' There was a pause while Freddy presumably did just that. 'See, I told you I was on the level . . . What do you care where I got it from?'

Leila was enjoying the pastry. It was some kind of raspberry and honey number. Mac continued. 'I've got it, that's all that matters, right? Just give me two hundred on the Red Sox.'

The Red Sox were up against Oakland. Oakland's hitters were good against lefties and the Sox were starting a lefty. Mac was a born loser. Leila licked her lips and continued to the make-up area where Consuela was burning something in a little dish that smelled of sandalwood and sent out pink smoke. Cassandra, the make-up girl, looked curious. 'What are you doing?' she asked.

Consuela fanned the flames. 'Chasing off the evil spirits.'

'This movie sure needs it. First Tommy gets run into, then the writer's cat gets stolen. The movie is jinxed.' Cassandra looked at Leila. 'All we'd need is Leila to snap a leg –' Cassandra broke a crisp pretzel as she said it, sending a shock wave through Leila – 'and we're toast.'

Leila was totally superstitious and what Cassandra said immediately got to her. Maybe the movie was jinxed? Leila would be wrapping herself in cotton wool. No more trips through the Hollywood Hills, thank you. Leila spun around three times while singing in her head the words to a Britney Spears song backwards. It was something her pal Paris had been overheard to say brought good luck and, given what Paris had achieved with minimal talent, Leila figured it was a worth a shot. The amazing thing was that Britney's songs actually made more sense backwards than forwards.

The spinning, however, made Leila dizzy and she

stumbled straight into the food cart and sent the turkey wraps flying.

'We are cursed!' somebody called out.

'This is the *Macbeth* of movies,' muttered another.

Leila's attempts at getting rid of the hex hadn't exactly proved successful.

'Leila, you okay?'

It was Charlotte, hurrying over.

'Yeah, I'm fine,' Leila whispered.

'You're wobbling all over the place.'

'Hey, you should have seen me when Aerosmith used to party at Chateau Marmand.'

Charlotte's attention was stolen by Sarah-Jane heading right towards her. She did not seem happy.

'Don't think I don't know what your game is.'

Charlotte looked around to see if she was talking to anybody else.

'I'm talking to *you*, Kangaroo Jill.'

'My name is Charlotte.'

Charlie wanted to be polite but there were limits. She noted Sarah-Jane's entourage already beginning to move towards them in a wave.

'Think you're pretty special getting yourself that trailer with a pizza oven, plasma and phone lines, don't you?'

'It was nothing to do with me.'

Sarah-Jane jabbed a finger at her. 'Darn right it was nothing to do with you. I'm the star, got it? I'm the kid in Leila's life. You keep away from my turf.'

Before Charlotte could reply, Sarah-Jane turned on her heel and started towards her minders, publicists and flunkeys.

'Oh, go blow it out your butt, midget-brain,' snapped Leila.

Sarah-Jane turned slowly and began to advance again on Charlotte. 'What did you say?'

Charlotte could tell the truth, which was 'nothing', but then it might seem like she'd backed down. And Charlotte never backed down. 'You heard.'

She was again aware of Leila's annoying line about lies being part and parcel of Hollywood.

Sarah-Jane was stunned. 'Fine. You want to be fired, congratulations, you got your wish.'

'You can't fire me.'

Charlotte and Sarah-Jane were now nose to nose. The hangers-on were standing there, listening to every word, stunned that somebody would talk to Sarah-Jane the way they wished they could.

Sarah-Jane smiled thinly. 'I'll get Mr Gold to fire you.'

Charlotte was unmoved. 'He can't fire me either. I'm here at the request of Leila's owner. You lose me, you lose Leila. And we all know how well your last picture did without her, don't we?'

There as an audible intake of collective breath behind her that seemed to make Sarah-Jane's skin pucker. She had been stopped in her tracks. Her finger shook with anger. 'Just stay out of my way.'

For the second time she fled, her groupies rushing behind her.

Leila let out a low whistle. 'Got to say, Charlie, you could really make it in this town.'

Charlotte had found the whole thing unpleasant. 'Come on. Let's get you back for the action run through.'

As they started back they found one of the gaffers handing out lucky rabbits' feet to his cronies. Leila explained how everybody thought the movie was jinxed.

'There's no hex, it's just coincidence,' said Charlotte firmly.

'You've got some nasty scratches there,' came a voice to their left. They turned to see the first aid nurse nodding at the arm of one of Tommy's assistants.

'Brambles got me,' he replied.

'Well, I'd better put some antiseptic cream on,' said the nurse. 'Way this movie is going you'll end up with bubonic plague.'

Charlotte met Leila's gaze with more assurance than she felt.

'It's in their heads,' she said. 'There's no curse on the movie.'

ɔ ɔ ɔ ɔ

'It's like there's a curse on this movie,' said a worried Joel Gold later as he stood on the porch and watched the last of the crew peel away. Hector Martinez and Hawthorne shared his gloomy expression as they sipped iced tea with Strudworth. Charlotte and Leila were on lemonade.

'Caroline,' Mr Gold nodded at Strudworth, 'wondered if anybody might have taken Oscar to hurt Honey.'

'Deliberately took him?' Martinez's face curled in doubt.

'A cat-snatcher?' Hawthorn infected the word with incredulity.

Strudworth distanced herself. 'It was actually Charlotte's idea.'

Charlotte went red with embarrassment.

'Everybody likes Honey,' said Martinez.

'Everybody,' echoed Hawthorn.

'A jilted boyfriend perhaps?' suggested Strudworth.

All three men shook their heads.

'Not Honey,' said Joel Gold.

'Every inch the spinster,' said Martinez.

Hawthorn didn't comment, just shook his head.

'Still,' added Mr Gold, 'it was an idea. In fact, Charlotte, you've been so helpful I thought you might like to take in Excelsior Studios tonight.'

'Thanks, but I should keep Leila exercised.'

'Take her with you,' said Martinez. 'After the studio closes to the public why don't you go over for a look? You can go wherever you please. Hawthorn will meet you, right Hawthorn?'

'Yes, sir!'

Mr Gold wagged a finger, 'But don't stay out too late. Tomorrow is the first day of shooting and we need Leila fresh.'

ↄ ↄ ↄ ↄ

After dinner they hitched Leila's float to the limousine and Fernando drove them across to Excelsior Studios. Miss Strudworth was meeting up with some former 'combatants' as she called them – riders who she had competed against in her heyday – so she did not join them. They entered via a special gate where Hawthorn was waiting. He showed Fernando where to park and handed a pass and map to Charlotte.

'Just start here and work your way up to Main Street,' he said. 'Anything you want to see. Unfortunately I have a lot on with the movie starting shooting tomorrow and can't stay.'

Charlotte thanked him, told Fernando to expect them back in about an hour, mounted Leila and trotted off.

It was a warm night and the studio lots were well lit. They trotted past the empty 'train', which during working hours carried patrons around the various locations. Leila was animated. 'First stop, the popcorn fountain.'

Charlotte allowed Leila to lead her to the fountain that was in the shape of a small rocket on a launch pad.

'Put your pass in,' ordered Leila.

Charlotte did as she was told, sliding her pass into the slot. Immediately a giant bucket appeared beneath the rocket. Moments later, popcorn gushed into the bucket until it was overflowing.

'Way to go, Charlie. Now, the Terror-tory.'

This, as it turned out, was an area devoted to the studio's very successful horror movies, especially *Suckers*, which was about a rampant giant squid that had featured in three smash movies.

'Can't catch me, can't catch me!' taunted Leila as the giant mechanical tentacles swung this way and that. They took a tunnel into an aquarium area filled with real sharks, fish and stingrays. It was a little spooky with nobody else around, but for Charlotte, who had never seen the ocean up close and had never been underwater, it was breathtaking. Leila finished off the popcorn and hustled them out to the backlots. They rode through Gulch Valley, a series of sets made to look like a western town. It reminded Charlotte of Snake Hills. Cardboard gunslingers suddenly appeared in windows and from behind carts and began firing strawberry-flavoured paintballs. Leila made sure Charlotte got hit plenty. Charlotte enjoyed dodging as the balls powered towards her. From there it was onto the mechanical Pirate Ship which 'sailed' from one side of the lake to the other. Actually the ship ran on tracks under the water but the effect was just as if you were sailing on an ocean. Particularly enjoyable was the lemonade 'monsoon', where lemonade rained down upon you. Ponchos and hats were provided to keep your clothes dry. Leila, of course, refused either. They worked their way through the amusement park, Leila having a great laugh on the carousel, where she posed as a wooden horse. They got off the carousel and headed for the main street.

Leila nodded at a large white building. 'This was the university I attended in *Horses for Courses*. During the day it's actually where the accountants work. And here is the Leila pavilion!' Leila nodded proudly at the building which was shaped like the rear end of a horse. The entry door was behind a large tail that swished from side to side.

Charlotte giggled.

'What's so funny?'

Charlotte pointed. 'The entry ramp. We walk up your backside.'

Leila was miffed. 'It was supposed to be the exit but the builder was dyslexic and got it round the wrong way. Anyway, what does it matter? Come on.'

Leila trotted up into what was essentially a living museum to Leila and Sarah-Jane. Made to look something like the inside of a barn, there were costumes and props from their movies and large screens showing selections of favourite scenes. There was Leila in glasses in the lecture theatre for *Horses for Courses*, Sarah-Jane leaping from Leila onto another speeding horse in *Thrills and Spills* and Sarah-Jane playing a young Russian gymnast who overhears a plot to assassinate the U.S. President, defects to the U.S. and becomes a champion equestrienne in *Dressage to Kill*.

In the centre of the pavilion was a small ring.

'This was the set for *Dressage to Kill*. And over there is the train we had to leap onto during *Hot to Trot*.'

Of course it wasn't a real train locomotive but it looked like one. By the time they had done the pavilion it was time to start back. Whereas before there had been a few staff visible, the place was now deserted.

'This is real fun,' said Leila as they approached Disaster Zone. 'Especially the simulated earthquake. Press this button.'

Charlotte did as she was told, pressing a button that started the attraction. Gradually a loud rumbling began and the ground beneath their feet started shaking. Leila giggled.

'Fun, eh?'

But Charlotte found it a little nerve-racking, especially when the buildings began to sway.

'Just like the real thing, eh?' said Leila.

Charlotte's eyes travelled to a pen full of stacked oil drums high behind them on top of a small hill.

'Don't worry, nothing happens.'

'They look like real drums.'

'They *are* real drums but the barrier keeps them . . .'

As Leila spoke the barrier holding the drums broke. A sea of drums cascaded towards them. For an instant the two were spellbound. Then they reacted in sync. Leila accelerated from stationary to a gallop in the blink of an eye. Charlotte drove her on.

'Come on!'

The drums bounced down the hill, relentlessly pursuing them. Leila powered on, the noise of thundering drums like a herd of cattle. Charlotte threw a look behind her. The drums were gaining by the second. The pirate ship lay ahead of them at the end of the landing pier in the man-made lake. Charlotte knew it was their only hope. Even Leila couldn't outrun the drums.

'Jump!' She dug in her heels.

Leila yelled, 'Are you crazy?' but she trusted Charlotte with her life. Charlotte looked back to see drums licking Leila's heels. They had to make the ship. Leila gave it everything. It was the longest jump she'd ever had to do, the entire length of the small pier. It was a well-timed take-off, the trajectory was looking good. But there was a problem. The ship had started to leave the pier.

Chapter 7

Leila couldn't believe her eyes. The ship was sailing away and she had already jumped for where she thought it would be. She stretched her body to the max, every sinew lengthening like a rubber band. She was dropping, the water rushing towards her . . .

Thump.

She landed on the aft deck and skidded to a halt. Charlotte swung back. Drums hit the end of the small pier and flew through the air like rocks from a catapult . . . zeroing in on the stern of the sailing ship.

Plop, plop, plop!

The drums tumbled into the water just a metre from the ship's rudder, hitting so hard they sprayed Charlotte with water. She breathed a massive sigh of relief as the boat pulled away. Had the ship not been moving they would have been sunk. Literally.

Fernando was waiting for them at the car. He listened in disbelief at what Charlotte told him.

'The barrier broke? Wow, this movie really *is* jinxed.'

Fernando immediately got on the phone to Mr Gold and reported the incident to him. A trembling Hawthorn was waiting for them at the gate when they arrived. He looked sickly white, as if he had rolled himself in flour.

'Mr Martinez called me. Mr Gold had called him. I'm so sorry. I'll look into it and fire the idiot responsible. If Leila had been injured . . .'

Hawthorn let out a low whistle, as if that outcome would be too impossible to contemplate.

'Not to mention Charlotte here,' put in Fernando, glowering.

'Of course, of course. Too horrible to contemplate.'

Charlotte had a fair idea Hawthorn was really only concerned for his job. He clapped his hands together, striving for a cheery manner.

'Well, sleep tight and see you on set tomorrow.'

Miss Strudworth was still out with her friends but Joel Gold was waiting for them in the driveway on their return. He was very nice to Charlotte, having ordered a hot chocolate for her in advance. While he listened to her account, he checked Leila all over.

'I don't know what we've done to get the fates against us,' he said sadly. 'But the most important thing is that you and Leila are okay. Try to get a good night's sleep.'

A surprise was waiting for them in their trailer – Feathers, swinging on a perch watching the latest MTV video clips.

'Hey, guys, how was the studio?' he asked, strutting along his perch, playing air guitar with his wings.

Leila laughed cynically. 'Fabulous. If you want to be a tenpin at Dewey's bowling alley with a thousand balls coming at you.'

They gave Feathers the run-down. He shook his head. 'I'm glad I'm not on this picture. It really is doomed.'

Leila became depressed.

'Guys, if anything happens to me, tell my mom I'm sorry if I ever let her down.'

'Nothing's going to happen while I'm with you,' said Charlotte. She clicked off the TV, much to Feathers' dismay.

'Right now we need to sleep and feel fresh in the morning. The movie is going to be fine.'

Though she wasn't sure if she truly believed that.

Charlotte woke at the crack of dawn. Leila and Feathers were both still snoring as she showered, dressed and left the trailer to find the big prime mover arriving to tow them to the location. Strudworth, resplendent in jodhpurs and boots, had started the day with a brisk walk around the estate. Charlotte filled her in on the Excelsior Studios experience as the truck driver hooked up the trailer.

'Had you been injured, I never would have forgiven myself,' said Strudworth.

'Fortunately I wasn't. We're both fine.'

Strudworth's face wrinkled into a sad frown. 'Perhaps this whole thing is wrong. Perhaps I should have just sold up Thornton Downs and gone to work for somebody else.'

'No way,' said Charlotte so vociferously that she surprised even herself. 'My dad always said that when we overcome setbacks, it makes us even stronger.'

Strudworth laid a hand on Charlotte's shoulder. 'Charlotte Richards, you remind me of myself when I was your age. When we get older though, we lose a little confidence in our ability to change the world.'

'What would Zucchini have done if he had fallen at the steeple?'

Strudworth's eyes clouded at the thought of that

most magnificent of horses which it had been her honour to partner.

'He would have got straight back up. You're right, Charlotte. This is no time to wallow in self-doubt or pity. Tally-ho!' Strudworth raised an imaginary whip in the air and strode to her bungalow. A bleary-eyed Leila poked her head from the trailer.

'What time is it?'

'Showtime,' replied Charlotte.

The location for the day's shoot was the Botanical Gardens at Griffith Park, not too far from Mr Gold's house. The thick plants and dense undergrowth was to pass as Brazilian rainforest. Charlotte was surprised to find how long it took the crew to set up their lights and cameras even though they all seemed to be moving furiously. Tommy Tempest flitted from one area to another checking on progress. Zara arrived, her arms laden with really groovy pink sports bags featuring the famous horseshoe logo of all the Leila merchandise.

'You want one?'

'Oh, wow, can I?' said Charlotte. She wasn't used to people giving things to her.

'Of course. It's for the media and a couple of select gals like Sarah-Jane and yourself.'

'Thank you so much, Zara.'

'No trouble, Charlotte.'

Zara moved off. Charlotte looked inside the bag to find Sarah-Jane perfume, some chocolate bars with Leila's face on the wrapper, and a bunch of postcards, which had 'Welcome from the set of Leila's latest movie' written over them. Charlotte was rapt – they would be perfect for writing to her dad and Hannah. A girl's loud whining voice dragged Charlotte's attention to wardrobe. Sarah-Jane was giving Henrietta hell.

'I don't like it. It's ripped,' she said, throwing away the khaki shirt Henrietta had selected for her.

'Of course it's ripped. You're supposed to have been tracking the wildlife smugglers through thick jungle for five days.'

'Maybe I carry a spare?'

Henrietta sought Tommy's decision.

'Sarah-Jane, wear the agreed wardrobe,' said Tommy, knowing his day would be full of this arbitration. Charlotte had no intention of getting within Sarah-Jane's orbit today. Feathers flew over and perched on her shoulder.

He yawned. 'First week is always like this. Sarah-Jane and Leila especially. Throwing tantrums to see who gets the most attention.'

Charlotte said to Feathers, 'I really think Leila has matured. She'll be better this time.'

Feathers chuckled. 'You can take the star out of Hollywood but when you bring her back – careful, you might still have a problem child.'

ᗡ ᗡ ᗡ ᗡ

At that moment Leila was rummaging through the spice rack in the trailer's kitchenette. Aha, that's what she wanted . . . Fresh chilli. She tipped the jar so it rolled off the bench and onto the floor. She picked up a tea towel in her teeth, dropped it over the jar and then slammed down her hoof in one short, sharp motion, hearing the crack of breaking glass with satisfaction. She removed the tea towel and lifted out two fat chillies, which she ground underfoot while humming a song by the Red Hot Chili Peppers – a little bit of thought association there. She looked down at the resultant red paste, knowing what she as a star was required to do next, distasteful as it might be. She bent down and sniffed.

Oh! That got her. Like snorting dynamite. She felt her eyes, nose and throat swell and burn. Her nose began running and her eyes dribbled tears.

Great!

At the make-up trailer, Sarah-Jane thrashed about in the chair.

'No, I hate that, it looks horrible. I don't want kohl all over my face.' She tried to rub it off but her limbs were restrained by leather bands. 'You can't do this to me, Cassandra.'

Cassandra was immune to the threats. She gobbled an almond croissant and licked her fingers with an air of superiority.

'Mr Tempest said I could do whatever was necessary to make it look like you'd been hiding in a jungle for five days. The kohl makes it look like dirt but I suppose I could get real dirt . . .'

'I'll kill Tommy,' bellowed Sarah-Jane.

Cassandra chuckled. 'Then you'll wind up in one of these for real.'

The 'these' she referred to was the chair, actually an electric chair designed for execution, which had been in reserve at a penitentiary before the State had abandoned capital punishment. Tommy poked his head in but wisely stayed in the doorway.

'Everything to your liking, I hope, Sarah-Jane?'

'You wait, Tommy. I'll blog you so bad you'll wish you'd never set eyes on me.'

Tommy already wished that but he kept it to himself. A concerned Zara appeared at his shoulder.

'Hate to bother you, Tommy. It's Leila. I think she has a cold.'

Tommy groaned and headed off. Sarah-Jane's screams echoed behind him. 'Tommy! Tommy, you come back here. I need you to help with my motivation.'

Charlotte was watching the camera crew set up when Tommy strode past. He stopped when he saw her and she could see he was anxious.

'Was Leila okay this morning?'

'Fine.'

'Looks like she has a cold.'

Charlotte immediately sprinted after Tommy towards the trailer. Feathers, who had caught the eye of a pretty macaw in the rainforest canopy and was just doing a little flirtatious feather-puffing, was torn. He wanted to stay – the bird had amazing plumage – but reluctantly he decided duty came first and gave wing after Charlotte.

Tommy opened the door and walked in to find Leila lying on the floor, eyes red, sniffling. Charlotte's heart sank when she saw her. The movie *was* cursed!

As Tommy went over to see Leila, Charlotte caught Feathers' wink. Charlotte understood. Leila wasn't sick at all. This was a ruse for sympathy.

'How's my best girl? Have you got a cold, Leila?'

Leila nodded sadly and let out a few more tears. It was as easy as stamping your hoof print in playdough. Humans were so easy to fool. She saw Charlotte appear behind Tommy, fold her arms and narrow her eyes at Leila. Oh-oh. Looked like she'd tumbled. A worried Tommy glanced up at Charlotte.

'You think she's going to need the vet?'

Leila almost whimpered, laying it on thick.

Charlotte said, 'I'm not sure. It could just be she has some allergy.'

What was the kid playing at? Leila turned to Tommy, shook her head and snorted through her nostrils as if to say how wrong Charlotte was.

Tommy was distressed. 'I think she's got a bad cold.'

Leila smirked at Charlotte. Gotcha.

Charlotte didn't flinch. 'If she has a cold then she won't be able to eat all day.'

Leila shot back a fierce look. The little minx! Why didn't she just butt out of what didn't concern her?

'Just a second,' said Charlotte. She poked her head out of the trailer and saw one of the kitchenhands walking past with a tray of fresh doughnuts. 'May I?'

She brought three of them back. 'If she doesn't eat this pineapple and chocolate doughnut –' she said, laying it on thick – 'then I guess she really *is* sick.'

Tommy was stroking Leila. Charlotte placed one of the doughnuts in front of her. Leila fought her natural instinct to gobble it even though her saliva glands were already bubbling. Charlotte took a bite of one of the others and made a deep sound in her throat.

'Yum, these fresh doughnuts are so scrummy they melt in your mouth.'

That was it. Leila couldn't resist. She snaffled the doughnut in front of her in one gulp.

Tommy laughed. 'You were right, Charlotte. I think she was just foxing for a little TLC. Leila, you're a peach but you're no better than Sarah-Jane. Now come on, I want you ready to shoot in ten minutes.'

As soon as he was gone Leila stood, indignant.

'That was despicable. Interfering in my manipulation of the director.'

'Tommy doesn't need any more stress,' barked Feathers, thinking about that pretty macaw back there.

'You mind your own business too, no-neck. You guys don't understand. This is a war between Sarah-Jane and me. You blink, you're dead.'

Leila scoffed a second doughnut.

'You don't seem too dead to me,' quipped Charlotte. 'Why don't you two just do what you're being paid a lot of money to do: your job.'

'That,' spluttered Leila through a mouthful of mush, 'would be setting a very dangerous precedent.'

Leila didn't let on but she was extremely nervous waiting, as Cassandra touched up her make-up before her first scene. It wasn't a particularly taxing scene but it required substantial wardrobe as Leila had to be camouflaged under leaves. In the scene Sarah-Jane was supposed to be looking through binoculars at the smugglers on a far ridge while, unbeknown to her, one snuck up behind her. Leila was to emerge from the trees where she'd been hiding and bump him over. A year ago Leila would have thought nothing of that. But a lot can change in a year.

'Talent on set,' the first assistant director called out.

Charlotte entered and took Leila by the bridle.

'Wish me luck,' whispered Leila.

'You don't need it. You're a star.'

Charlotte kissed her on the neck and sent her forward under the hot lights. Leila positioned herself among the foliage. A leaf poked her in the eye. She had forgotten how uncomfortable this acting gig could be.

Strudworth was sitting in a steamer chair with Joel Gold, who enthused over the way Leila had settled into her position.

'That's what we love about Leila. It's like she has read the script herself.'

Charlotte was excited as she took her spot behind them and watched the clapperboard girl slam the little board down with a slap.

'Action,' called Tommy.

Leila was trembling as Sarah-Jane did her binocular bit. Next came the bad guy up behind her . . . okay now! Her legs almost wouldn't work but once she stepped into that hot light nothing else existed. Leila was in the moment. She stepped out, did her famous Leila shimmy where she crossed her back legs in a macarena-like move, then butted the startled smuggler onto his backside. Sarah-Jane turned, her mouth forming a surprised zero, her eyes wide as a jumbo jet's wingspan. The smuggler pretended to try to get to his feet.

'Not so fast, Cheese-ball,' admonished Sarah-Jane, which was Leila's cue to plant a hoof in the smuggler's chest. The smuggler writhed about convincingly.

'Please, get the devil tree off me,' cried the spineless smuggler.

Sarah-Jane snapped her fingers and Leila desisted.

Sarah-Jane quickly wrapped the smuggler in strong vine.

'Hear that, Leila? Now you're a devil tree.'

'Cut,' came Tommy's voice. Then to the assembled crowd, 'Everybody . . . she's back.'

The whole cast and crew began to applaud. Joel Gold stood in his chair. Leila listened to it and drank it in. Hooray for Hollywood!

Charlotte happened to glance over the crowd and notice there was one exception to the celebration. Sarah-Jane was giving a baby clap with two fingers. Charlotte didn't need to be told that Leila had won the first round.

ↄ ↄ ↄ ↄ

The shoot proceeded without incident up to lunch, which was Leila's favourite part of any shoot. She stamped impatiently by the trailer waiting for the kitchen staff to bring over a variety of pizzas.

'It's not a particularly healthy diet,' commented Charlotte, who was eating rice and vegetables.

'That's what I've been saying for years,' added Feathers.

'I'm having *salad* with the pizza, aren't I?' shot back Leila.

'I don't think that's how it works,' said Charlotte. A familiar figure came towards them. Honey Grace still seemed agitated.

'Just thought I'd drop in to see how it's going,' she said.

'So far so good. Any news about Oscar?'

Honey shook her head sadly. 'I was so disappointed that pussy wasn't him. I still can't sleep. I tried to write but in four hours all I managed was this.' She produced a page which had no more than two lines written on it. 'I've told Mr Gold to hire another writer.'

Leila groaned.

Charlotte asked whether the Grants had been in touch about the window cleaner.

'Oh yes, I forgot you didn't know. My brain is all over the place. They didn't organise any cleaning.'

'Is there anybody you think might have a grudge against you?' asked Charlotte.

'What do you mean?' Honey was confused by the question.

Charlotte elaborated. 'Perhaps somebody stole Oscar to hurt you.'

Honey was dismayed by the thought. 'I don't know that many people and those I do are my friends. I did yell at a man once who nearly ran me over.'

Charlotte was thinking that whoever took Oscar, if indeed anybody had, would have to know a fair bit about Honey.

'If somebody did take Oscar, I only hope it was because he is such a lovely cat and they wanted to spoil him.' It was clear she was fighting back tears. 'Anyway, I just wanted to thank you again, Charlotte, for all your concern and to wish Leila well.' She checked her watch. 'I'd best be off now.'

'You're not staying?'

'I have an appointment with a counsellor who helps people grieving.'

Honey shuffled off, her whole body bowed.

'Seeing a shrink, that's bad,' said Leila. But she brightened as the tray of pizzas headed her way. She demolished them in no time.

'I wonder what S-J will try?' She licked her lips for the last taste of oregano.

'What do you mean?'

Feathers picked at a piece of crust and explained. 'It's day one. So far Leila has been the star. Sarah-Jane will have to do something to get the attention back on her.'

Leila stood waiting for her cue. The scene was a tricky one. It entailed Leila starting to canter when she heard Sarah-Jane's alarm whistle. Sarah-Jane would then burst out of the bushes, supposedly on the run from pursuing bad guys, run alongside Leila, and haul herself onto the saddle. By the time she grabbed the reins, Leila needed to be in full gallop. The bad guys then emerged from the bushes and fired after them. Not real bullets of course. Blanks. The clapperboard clapped. Tommy's voice floated over from the truck where he was sitting behind the cameraman.

'And action.'

Leila waited. There was the whistle. She started forward, trying to judge her speed just right. Sarah-Jane burst out of the trees and ran alongside her. She reached for the saddle, got her foot in the stirrup . . .

'Aeee,' she yelled. 'She's going too fast.'

Leila knew that wasn't in the script. Sarah-Jane's weight melted away, there was a cloud of dirt and Tommy's voice yelled, 'Cut'.

Leila pulled up immediately and looked over to see Sarah-Jane writhing on the ground. Tommy had jumped down from the truck and people were swarming from all over the place. Leila immediately suspected it was a con job.

'Are you all right?'

Tommy knelt beside Sarah-Jane, who was massaging her ankle.

'I–I'm not sure.' She turned and pointed accusingly at Leila. 'She was going way too fast.'

'Can you stand?' asked Joel Gold.

Leila stewed as Sarah-Jane did a great impression of somebody who'd just had their foot chomped off by an alligator. Her bottom lip quivered, she clutched Mr Gold and, with enormous 'bravery', hauled herself up. The doctor, a handsome young guy in jeans and sweatshirt, had arrived with his bag.

'Let's have a look.' He reached to Sarah-Jane's boot but she immediately shrieked, 'Agh, agh, agh. Don't touch it.'

The doctor examined it as best he could and pronounced no obvious break.

That's a surprise, thought Leila.

'All the same, I'd better get her to the hospital for an X-ray.'

Leila watched the press gallery reach for their phones. This was going to make news. Sarah-Jane caught Leila's eye and Leila could detect a glint of triumph in her look.

'It was going so well. We'll have to wrap for the day.' Tommy sounded like he'd been kicked in the stomach.

Mr Gold sighed. 'This movie is cursed. Hector's going to have a seizure.'

Which is when Miss Strudworth's imperious voice drew attention to herself.

'I know nothing about making films, of course, but I'm sorry, Joel, I don't quite understand the problem.'

Mr Gold was patient. 'Sarah-Jane has hurt her ankle and there's no time to set up for another scene, so we have to finish for the day.'

'I'm so, so sorry,' offered Sarah-Jane.

'It's not your fault,' said Tommy.

'I know. It's Leila's,' she added with bite.

Leila had a good mind to stomp on her and really give her an injury.

Miss Strudworth persisted. 'Yes, I understand that. But are you doing close-ups?'

'It doesn't matter,' said Tommy. 'Sarah-Jane's the only one here who can do the stunt.'

'We normally have a stunt double,' explained Joel Gold, 'but that part of the budget had to be pared back to allow for us to shoot again when Honey . . . if Honey . . . finishes the script.'

'Charlotte can do it,' said Strudworth.

Leila cackled inside. Yes! Way to go, Struddy-Duddy. She shot a look at Sarah-Jane, whose eyes were darting as she tried to think of a block.

'It's a great idea but I'm afraid the union wouldn't be agreeable to that,' she said.

Joel Gold's face creased in rare joy. 'She's a member. I took out a membership for her so there'd be no problem with her being on set.'

Standing some metres away, Charlotte was aware of none of this conversation. When all eyes turned in her direction she looked behind her to see what they were looking at. There was nothing there. By the time she had turned back, Strudworth, Tommy Tempest and Joel Gold were looming.

'Guess what, Charlotte?' said Miss Strudworth.

'You're about to be in a movie,' smiled Joel Gold.

Charlotte's legs went weak.

'I – I don't understand . . .' she stammered.

'Look at that,' cracked Tommy. 'An actor already.'

Chapter 8

'You know, my ankle might not be as bad as I thought.'

Sarah-Jane went hobbling after Tommy as he neared the wardrobe area where Charlotte was being fitted out. Leila noted that it seemed to alternate between Sarah-Jane's left and right foot as to which one was 'injured'.

'No, we can't take a risk with you,' said Tommy firmly. 'If we had to stop the film because you were hurt, the insurance people would have grounds to halt any payout. You should go to the hospital for that X-ray.'

Leila sauntered over to Feathers, who was also delighted by the scene unfolding. 'Worst thing for her is that the press gallery has forgotten all about her. They want to see "Crocodoll Dundee" do her thing.' She nodded to where various media types were on their mobile phones and Blackberries, filing reports.

At the wardrobe trailer, Charlotte was extremely

nervous. Henrietta put her into Sarah-Jane's back-up wardrobe.

'You're almost exactly the same size.'

'In everything except ego,' whispered Cassandra, biting on a pretzel.

'How's she doing?' asked Tommy.

'Almost there,' said Henrietta.

'I don't have to say any lines, do I?' asked Charlotte.

'No, not in this scene, Charlotte.' Tommy was very reassuring. 'Just pretend it's you and Leila having fun.'

The first assistant director called out to Tommy that everybody was standing by.

'Okay, let's go, Charlotte,' said Tommy.

'Thank you, Henrietta.'

'It's a pleasure, Charlotte. I hope we do it again,' smiled Henrietta.

Charlotte's legs were jelly as she walked through the gallery of faces peering at her with a variety of emotions: curiosity in the case of the press; fondness in the case of Strudworth; animosity in the case of Sarah-Jane. She almost snarled at Charlotte but had no chance to say anything as she was suddenly hoisted in the air by paramedics and carried towards the ambulance.

Tommy led Charlotte into her position in the bushes where the second assistant director, Kansas, a big burly man, was waiting, headset clamped on.

'Kansas will cue you when to whistle and run for Leila. Now don't worry if we have to do this a few times; it's a very hard stunt, we know that.'

Charlotte nodded. Her mouth and throat were dry.

Tommy disappeared back out through the bushes.

'You're going to be fine, kid,' said Kansas.

Charlotte's life flashed before her as she tried to make sense of how she, a shy girl from the deep Australian outback, had wound up here in Holly-wood. She supposed it all had to do with Leila. Life could never be normal when she was around.

'And . . . action,' came Tommy's voice from beyond the trees. Kansas gestured for Charlotte to whistle. Which she did. Kansas listened to his headphones and nodded for Charlotte to go.

Charlotte burst out of the trees and ran towards Leila, who was moving across an open expanse of grass at a canter. While Charlotte had never done anything like this stunt with Leila, many times when she had been on a cattle drive with her father she had needed to mount her horse quickly to chase down a bolting steer. She reached Leila, threw out her hand, seized the pommel, and pulled herself into the saddle, not even bothering with stirrups as she galloped away hard. It was only when she approached the third assistant director waving her to stop that she remembered this was a movie stunt. She had lost herself completely in the moment. She pulled Leila to a halt.

'Nice job, Charlie,' said Leila from the side of her mouth. Tommy's truck came alongside.

'You didn't use the stirrups.' Tommy seemed quite confused.

Charlotte felt like an idiot. 'I'm so sorry. I can do it again. It's just that it slows you down and if I had men chasing me with guns I wouldn't bother.'

'No, no, no, it's great!' Tommy looked to his cameraman, who gave a thumbs up to show he'd captured it all. 'You were terrific, Charlotte. That's a take.'

People began to applaud.

'You know,' said Tommy's first assistant director arriving on the scene, 'we've still got a good hour. We could set up for another stunt.'

Tommy was nodding, his mind racing.

'The one where she gets caught by the creeper slung across the track and falls. If Sarah-Jane does it we'll be half a day fixing her hair.' He swung to Charlotte. 'What do you think, Charlotte? Think you could manage that?'

Charlotte shrugged. It was the kind of thing the kids from Snake Hills grew up doing – playing cowboys and indians, falling out of the saddle.

'Don't see why not, Tommy.'

Tommy suddenly had a spring in his step. 'Okay, guys, let's go.'

つ つ つ つ

'You really saved the day, Charlotte,' said Joel Gold later at a restaurant he had commandeered near the Kodak Theater in the heart of Hollywood. Miss Strudworth, Charlotte, Mr Gold and Leila were the only diners in the large room. Feathers had been most indignant that he was not allowed to come and Tommy was too busy planning shots for the next day.

'I don't think I did anything much.'

It wasn't false modesty from Charlotte. To her there was nothing easier than jumping on and off horses.

'Don't go getting too many ideas, Charlotte,' cautioned Strudworth. 'The Annie Oakley stunts belong on a movie set, not in the show ring.'

'Of course not, Miss.'

Charlotte was relishing her meal, steak with spaghetti and French fries. Leila was scoffing down vegetarian pasta.

'I've been coming to this place for forty-two years,' said Mr Gold affectionately as he looked around the room of somewhat faded splendour. 'Goran, the owner, began as a busboy the same time I started as a studio messenger. I used to have to pedal my bicycle from set to set passing on messages. Forty years ago, Caroline, what were you doing? Besides breaking boys' hearts, I mean?'

Leila groaned. The only thing worse than tetanus shots was being forced to watch Sarah-Jane's showreel or oldies flirting as they talked about ancient days. Okay if it were Mick Jagger and Marianne Faithful, maybe she could bear it, but Mr Gold and Strudworth. Yucch, it sent a shiver down her body.

Charlotte watched Miss Strudworth's smile creep over her face.

'I'm not sure there were too many boys with broken hearts, Joel.'

'Hey, Caroline, I can tell you were a stunner then, just as you are now.'

She melted. 'Well . . . there was one boy . . . Mark. He and I went to *The Sound of Music* together and then he was sent to Vietnam.' She shook her head sadly. 'I get upset every time I think of it.'

'He was hurt?' asked Mr Gold carefully.

'Oh no, he never even saw any action but he stopped off in Hong Kong and decided it was so much fun there he would stay. I never saw him again, though he did send a very nice postcard from Victoria Peak.'

Mr Gold's phone burst into life. 'Yes, Josh. How is she? That's great news . . . no, of course not, Charlotte was just filling in.'

He ended the call.

'Sarah-Jane's manager. X-ray was clear. She'll be fine for tomorrow.'

Of course she will, thought Leila. She's seen how expendable she is. Thirteen-year-old precocious brats are a dime a dozen. But try replacing a mare with attitude, a sense of rhythm and impeccable timing.

Goran, a small rotund man with black hair that looked like it may have been painted on, entered the room.

'Is everything to your liking?'

'The osso buco was marvellous,' smiled Strudworth.

'Steak is great,' added Charlotte.

'There is only one thing missing, my friend,' said Mr Gold with a serious expression.

Goran looked concerned.

'Where's Johan?'

Goran burst into a wide smile. 'You want some music, eh?'

'Could I request *The Sound of Music*?' Mr Gold asked.

Goran wagged a finger. 'Coming right up.'

He disappeared from the room in a flash.

'What's going on?' Caroline Strudworth had become quite girly in her manner.

'Just wait and see,' said Mr Gold, pouring her wine.

From outside the doorway came the sounds of violins. Two men and a woman dressed in gypsy-style costumes, the men with puffy shirts, cummerbunds and headbands, the woman in a flowing dress, entered playing.

Strudworth's hand fluttered to her heart.

Mr Gold leaned across, offering his hand. 'May I?'

'Of course.' Strudworth stood and the two prepared to dance, which was quite a sight with the small, portly Joel Gold and the tall, equine-like Strudworth.

'Perhaps Leila and I will go for a walk around,' suggested Charlotte.

'By all means,' said Joel Gold, gazing into Strudworth's eyes.

'Take your time,' said Miss Strudworth, gazing into his.

Leila and Charlotte left the room, watching them spin elegantly around the floor.

'Okay, Charlie, let's take in a little action, see if the pavement is cooking,' said Leila as they emerged from a side door into the street.

In Charlotte's home town of Snake Hills, a busy

night could be defined by more than a dozen cars lapping the town's one and only street. Charlotte had spent a night in the city once after running away from Thornton Downs but even that was nothing compared to this. There were so many people out and about. She couldn't get over the noise and motion, the giant billboards and endless stream of gleaming cars. Charlotte had thought people would be startled at a horse in their midst but, apparently, they were used to such sights and most barely offered a second glance. The sidewalk, as the Americans called it, was full of people in costumes doing little acts. Leila explained they were dressed like famous movie stars.

'Who is the little man with the funny moustache and the round hat?'

'The hat is called a bowler. That's supposed to be Charlie Chaplin.'

'Why do they dress up like them?'

'Why do you think?'

Charlotte saw some passing Chinese tourists place money in the bowler hat.

'They charge for it?'

'They don't charge. You pay if you want.'

Charlotte recognised the woman with the platinum blonde hair and the beauty spot.

'That's Marilyn Monroe, right?'

'Looks more like Marilyn Manson,' cracked Leila. She took a deep sniff of the gasoline fumes, the fried food and the desert dust that seemed to cling to the wind all over L.A.

'Hollywood Nights,' she said with a fondness, remembering how she had given Bob Seger the title for his famous song one night at the Sunset Marquee bar. Of course, he hadn't known it was her. He just heard somebody pass him and say, 'You should do a song about this, call it "Hollywood Nights".' He probably thought it was the cocktail waitress.

'Way to go, Leila,' called one young guy in a Lakers cap, from a passing car.

Leila nodded at a hotel. 'That's a famous rock'n'roll establishment where I've been for many an album launch.' She cackled. 'Should have seen Don Henley and me doing "Wild Horses" at the bar. That was something. Until Don decided to jump me through the plate glass window. Still don't know how I emerged without a scratch.'

A convertible went past loaded with young people who began tooting and screaming, 'Oh my God, it's Leila and Crocodoll Dundee!'

Leila showed off by rearing high.

Charlotte was flabbergasted. 'I was on TV for, like, five minutes.'

'That's all it takes,' said Leila knowingly.

'Don't worry though, by tomorrow you'll have been forgotten. Careful, you're about to step on Cary Grant.'

Charlotte's foot poised midstream. She looked down to see a gold star in the footpath. 'Oh, wow.'

'You get famous enough, you get your own star. I would have had mine by now if I hadn't stuck with you.'

A terrible thought snuck into Leila's brain. What if they gave Sarah-Jane a star and not her?

'Oh, look. I want to check this out.' Charlotte had spied a souvenir store that sold everything from small movie clapperboards to miniature Oscar statuettes. She dipped into her modest savings to make sure that her father and Hannah got something to remember her trip by. For her dad she bought a small plastic bust of Russ Raven. For Hannah she purchased a cap that read *Hollywood Heart-throb*. Leila was happy to see her friend so excited by her shopping spree.

'Now I'm going to show you the best site in Hollywood,' she promised and trotted off across the road. Charlotte was nearly run over three times following her. Leila had planted herself out front of a shop called The Ice-cream Emporium. Charlotte arrived just as the shop owner, a man with a thick moustache, broke into a huge smile and bellowed.

'Leila? Leila, you're back?'

Leila did a high whinny and rotated three-sixty degrees. A boy about twelve who had been waiting in line pulled out his iPod earphones.

'Is that really Leila?'

Leila nodded.

'Hey guys, it's Leila! You know – *Thrills and Spills*.'

Pretty soon a crowd had formed. Charlotte found herself jostled to the back but through the throng she was able to see Leila being handed a massive chocolate sundae by the owner.

'Settle down, everybody. You want a chance to pat Leila, you have to buy an ice-cream. Okay, who's first?'

There was a rush at the counter, people thrusting cash in the man's face. One old woman in a motorised wheelchair rammed the kids in front of her until they gave way.

Ↄ Ↄ Ↄ Ↄ

Later, as they headed back to the restaurant, Leila, her mouth stained with caramel and chocolate topping, filled Charlotte in.

'My pal Stavros has been running that shop for years. We have a nice little arrangement.'

'I saw. He gives you a massive sundae and you flutter your eyelashes for the customers.'

'It's the way Hollywood works. You scratch my back, I scratch yours. Speaking of which, how about when we get back you run the brush over my coat a few times?'

'What did your last slave die of?'

'She had to watch a complete hour of Sarah-Jane's screen tests.' Leila cackled and sighed with pleasure. 'That was so good today. She did the old sore ankle and whammy, it came back and bit her on the backside. Pity you can't act, Charlie. We could have fun.'

They were walking past a huge electrical shop with dozens of TV screens in the window when Charlotte stopped cold.

'Look, there's Todd!'

Leila looked at one of the big plasmas. Sure enough, that handsome stallion Warrior was clearing a jump. A caption came up: 'Live from San Diego'. Todd had only just started his round and they watched, glued, as Warrior cleared the hurdle, the water jump and, finally, the big steeple before reefing around and leaping another hurdle and coming back to the finish. Todd was the consummate rider. Charlotte watched, excited, as progressive points came up on the screen. He was now coming third overall. She felt a momentary pang. As much as today had been awesome, doing stunts, sharing sundaes right here in the swirling streets of Hollywood, she still missed her other life, the sun rising over Thornton Downs to the irritating laugh of kookaburras, the dry red earth of Snake Hills that caked your whole body . . . even mucking out the stables. She would enjoy this experience while it lasted but deep down Charlotte knew she did not want to be a star like Sarah-Jane.

∩ ∩ ∩

At that moment, not all that far from where Charlotte stood watching Todd, Sarah-Jane was sitting in her trailer in a funk. The day had been a disaster. That stupid Aussie girl had muscled in on her turf. Leila had received a standing ovation. It called for more drastic measures. Something to put Sarah-Jane back in the headlines where she belonged. Sarah-Jane's mind began humming. Hmm. Yes, that could do the trick.

Chapter 9

When Charlotte and Leila had returned to the restaurant they had found Strudworth and Mr Gold laughing and singing together. Their jollity had continued in the car.

'Caroline, you are so good for me. It helps me forget all the trouble I am in with this movie.'

'As my grandfather used to say, Joel, tears are wasted on ourselves.'

'I like that.'

'We must hope that Oscar turns up and, in the meantime, make sure that everything else runs smoothly.'

Mr Gold had Fernando drop them at the trailer. The next shooting day was in the same location but he and Miss Strudworth were staying at Mr Gold's.

'Thanks again, Charlotte. We'll see you on set tomorrow,' he called out as the car pulled away.

They found Feathers flaked out on the sofa, watching TV. Popcorn was strewn everywhere.

'What happened? You get Wolfmother over for a jam?' asked Leila, looking around at the mess.

Feathers snapped back. 'It was fine until I microwaved the popcorn. You ever tried to turn one of those things off with a wing? No, I guess not because *you* get to be taken out to restaurants, because *you* are the big stars and *you* don't care about your pal all alone back in the TRAILER.'

Charlotte felt sorry for him.

'I'm sorry, Feathers, but I tried. Mr Gold said you had to stay in.'

'You could have smuggled me in the trunk.'

Leila offered to blow hot air on his back to cheer him up. It was a particular favourite of his.

'Okay then, I suppose,' he said grudgingly.

'I'll tidy up,' offered Charlotte.

'They got a maid for that,' said Leila.

Charlotte wasn't going to leave it for a maid. She'd spent her life cleaning up after herself. She used a brush and pan to sweep up the popcorn. Among it she found a very colourful feather.

'This isn't yours, Feathers,' she stated, puzzled.

Feathers shifted guiltily. Leila seized on it. 'You've had company. You've been entertaining.'

'So?' said Feathers.

'So you make us feel guilty and get us blowing on

your feathers and all the time you've been canoodling
– no doubt with that macaw.'

'We weren't canoodling,' countered Feathers
stridently.

'Can-ood-ling,' taunted Leila.

'Take that back.' Feathers' voice had taken on a
shrieking quality.

'Can-ood . . . OW YOW!'

Feathers had fastened onto Leila's nose with his
beak. Charlotte had to intervene.

'Feathers, Leila, stop it. We have a big day
tomorrow.'

They finally broke apart.

'Feathers, up onto your perch. Leila, bed.'

A little while later after she had showered and
settled Leila under her gold horse blanket, Charlotte
turned off the light. She was soooo tired. Just as she
drifted off to sleep she heard Leila in an annoying
sing-song whisper, 'Canooooodling . . .'

'Shut up, long face,' snapped Feathers.

That was the last Charlotte remembered till morning.

Leila had been expecting Sarah-Jane to be difficult but
half the day was over and she still hadn't made a move.

Something was up. Sarah-Jane was never ever nice to the make-up girls. Could it be that she was worried Charlotte was so much better liked, she had decided to try to be nice to people for a change? Nah, not Sarah-Jane.

Charlotte had spent most of the morning cleaning tack. It was much more relaxing than the previous day. Everybody was very nice to her, even without her being on camera. Cassandra had even told her to pop into the trailer for a hair trim if she wanted. Zara came over to her, holding a sports bag.

'I think you left this at the breakfast tent.'

'Oh, sorry.'

'No problems.'

Charlotte felt foolish. She had thought she'd brought her bag back with her after breakfast. When she turned back to look at her trailer, there it was holding open her trailer door.

'Actually, it isn't mine,' she said but found that Zara was already running off on some other errand. Charlotte opened the bag and found a hairbrush, a toiletries bag, jeans, a jumper, pyjamas and a folded map of some sort. The clothes were her size but definitely not hers. Everything in here was brand new and designer label, which led to one obvious conclusion. The bag must belong to Sarah-Jane.

Great. If Sarah-Jane found her with this she'd accuse her of being a thief. Charlotte decided the easiest thing was to take it back and leave it by her trailer. Returning from there she heard a woman's high voice singing. The voice sounded extremely familiar. Strudworth? Singing?

Charlotte poked her head around a parked van and saw Miss Strudworth twirling and spinning as she sang, 'I could have danced all night.'

'Are you all right, Miss?'

Strudworth came back to earth but retained a beatific smile. 'All right? Oh I'm more than all right, Charlotte. I had the most wonderful evening last night. After we left you, Mr Gold and I danced on the terrace to all the big musicals: *South Pacific*, *The King and I*, *My Fair Lady*. That reminds me, he's invited us tonight to see the rushes.'

'What are they?'

'To tell you the truth, I'm not certain but I think it's the footage they shoot during the day or the day before.'

Charlotte was embarrassed. She'd forgotten that after doing the stunts they would actually wind up on film for everybody to see.

♪ ♪ ♪

That evening Charlotte's heart was in her mouth as she joined the select few filing into Mr Gold's personal theatrette. Charlotte noted Miss Strudworth had doused herself in perfume. Tommy Tempest was tired after a long day's shooting but relieved there had been no dramas. Leila had her own padded box from which to watch. The only other people there were Mr Gold and his and Tommy's assistants, Zara and the young man, who Charlotte remembered talking to the nurse about cleaning out his aunt's backyard. She now learned his name was Josh. Fernando doubled as projectionist. Feathers perched on Mr Gold's shoulder. Mr Gold sat beside Miss Strudworth.

'I'll watch with Leila,' said Charlotte, who really didn't want to be near people when they saw how awful she was on screen. Despite the long day of shooting, Leila was upbeat. She'd had massages and pedicures and the lunch cart had done one of her favourites, Chinese dim sum.

'Okay, Fernando, roll away,' called Joel Gold.

The lights dimmed in the theatre, which could seat around fifty people. Charlotte's heart was thumping. The film came onto a screen about twice the size of the big plasma in the trailer. Leila whispered that the rushes weren't treated or edited, it was just the raw footage. The first few minutes was taken up with scenes between Leila and Sarah-Jane. Then came the close-up of the bushes, which Charlotte knew would feature her. Her stomach tightened. She heard Tommy's voice, recorded on the day, calling 'action', and then she appeared, bursting out of the 'jungle' and running towards Leila, who had begun cantering. You couldn't tell it was her. The audience would assume it was Sarah-Jane. Charlotte watched herself leap up onto the moving Leila.

'Oh, love that shot!' clapped Tommy.

'Beau-tee-ful,' called Joel Gold.

Charlotte felt her face redden. She watched the shot of her galloping away on Leila. At the time she'd given no thought to the truck with the camera that had followed her but now she saw that it had been right behind her.

'Nice work,' whispered Leila. 'And will you look at those glutes!' She was admiring her own hindquarters as she galloped over the grass. They then watched the shot from a different camera angle to the side. Leila explained that Tommy would cut the two shots together to give the scene the most excitement.

Charlotte was more relaxed as she watched the rest of the stunts she had done. At the point where Charlotte had to ride into the vine slung across the track and fall off Leila, everybody spontaneously applauded.

'You're a natural, Charlotte,' called Tommy as the shot ended and Fernando clicked on the lights. 'Any time you want to do stunt work, call us.'

They all exited to the adjoining room where the kitchen staff were serving kebabs and mini pizzas. Feathers flew over and perched on Leila's head.

'Not bad, Charlie. I think you could have worked the camera a little more though.'

'Says you. No neck, no talent,' cracked Leila.

Charlotte was about to step into the breach when she noted the room suddenly hushing. She glanced over to the doorway where an ashen Mr Gold was talking to Zara.

'Call the police. They have to be notified.'

All eyes turned to him. With a grave voice he explained, 'I've just had a phone call from Sarah-Jane's minders. She's disappeared.'

Chapter 10

The room was enveloped in stunned silence, everybody being too shocked to move, except for Leila, who was eyeing off the chicken kebabs wondering how she could gobble them without skewering her mouth.

Strudworth was the first to speak. 'You mean she might have been kidnapped?'

Mr Gold nodded solemnly. 'Unfortunately, we have to assume that is a strong possibility. Apparently after wrapping today she went into a boutique on Melrose.'

That figured, thought Leila. Sarah-Jane was always buying some new designer frock or top or shoes. She turned back to the matter at hand. Maybe if she could stick one end of the kebab into something like a corkboard, she could slide the meat off the skewer with her mouth sideways? Humans just didn't consider that all horses had to work with was hooves.

Tommy was at a loss. 'But she has all those minders?'

Mr Gold explained. 'They waited while she went to try on a new outfit. Somebody could have been lurking in the change room for her and spirited her out the back alley.'

Leila gave up on the kebabs and snaffled a mini pizza instead.

'She hasn't gone to her parents?' asked Strudworth.

'They live in Colorado. They've heard nothing from her or from any kidnappers.' Mr Gold shook his head sadly.

'If anything happens to Sarah-Jane . . .' People nodded slowly as the grief Mr Gold felt made his tongue immobile. Miss Strudworth put her hand on his shoulder. He forced himself to speak the ugly words that finished his sentence, '. . . this movie is sunk.'

Charlotte was beginning to think the movie was, indeed, cursed.

Mr Gold announced he was going over to meet the police at the sight of the presumed abduction. Miss Strudworth announced she would go with him. Tommy suggested they should bring Leila. Mr Gold jumped at the idea.

'Yes, that special bond between them might enable Leila to pick up a scent or something.'

159

Leila, demolishing her third mini pizza, was piqued. What was she, a bloodhound? The only scent she was interested in was the scent of this very nice cannelloni here.

'Charlotte, you bring Leila to the float.'

Leila resisted Charlotte as best she could but was dragged out before she could snaffle one of the coconut pies. Just like that selfish brat Sarah-Jane to get herself abducted before Leila had eaten properly.

ↄ ↄ ↄ ↄ

The police had cordoned off the area on busy Melrose Avenue. Fernando pulled up out front and they all got out. Charlotte led Leila from her float. The night was instantly lit with the flashes of the waiting paparazzi. Somebody squealed out a greeting to Leila. A uniformed policeman approached Mr Gold, who did the talking and they were all waved through into the boutique. On the way in Charlotte spied the price tag on a bikini.

'They're a bargain, only eight twenty-five.'

Leila gave her the hard truth. 'Eight hundred and twenty-five, you mean.'

Charlotte gasped. 'Who would pay that much for a pair of swimmers?'

'Somebody who wanted to impress people by how much they could waste on swimmers?'

They had to clam up then because they were now inside the shop, which was quite cleverly designed so that it was like you were inside a giant pinball machine. Leila checked out the salesgirl. She looked like a model, slumming with regular work, batting her eyelashes at the handsome police officer questioning her. Sarah-Jane's two bodyguards were off to the side, being interviewed by a different police officer.

Leila edged up to eavesdrop on the salesgirl. 'I already told the other policeman . . .'

'Yes, but would you mind telling me?' said the good-looking cop.

The girl smiled. 'Be my pleasure. Sarah-Jane came in here and was browsing. I didn't hassle her. She's been in here before. If she wants something, she'll buy it. The bodyguards came and stood just about where you are.'

Which was in front of the counter.

'What happened then?'

'She found a little dress she liked and showed it to me like she was going to try it on.'

'And you started talking to the bodyguards?'

'Yeah, they're so well cut. I asked what gym they went to.'

Leila snorted. So the salesgirl is flirting with the bodyguards who are flirting with her. Nobody is looking at Sarah-Jane.

'Any other customers?'

'A few. Women coming in or out. But I didn't see any others go back to the change rooms.'

'You have security cameras for shoplifting?'

She shook her head. 'We can't afford a lawsuit from somebody saying we filmed them getting changed. The clothes have electronic tags. If they're not scanned, they beep when you leave the store.'

'Excuse me?'

Leila was surprised Charlotte had piped up. The policeman and salesgirl both turned to her like she had no right to breathe.

'Did Sarah-Jane have a bag with her?'

The salesgirl thought. 'Yes, I think so.'

'A pink sports bag about so long?'

The girl nodded. The policeman looked at Charlotte, as if asking a silent question.

'We were given them on set,' said Charlotte. The policeman made a note. The salesgirl snapped her fingers and suddenly became friendly.

'Thought I knew you. You're Crocodoll Dundee, right?'

Charlotte smiled.

Leila whinnied and threw her head around to make sure they noticed her.

'And Leila! Right.'

Charlotte asked if they could go through to the change room area and the cop waved them through.

'Why did you want to know about the bag?' whispered Leila.

'Tell you later,' said Charlotte.

In the change room area Mr Gold and Miss Strudworth were talking to a silver-haired detective. The change room wasn't really a room or rooms at all, just an empty three-sided box made of chipboard. Thick curtain material divided the box into two equal chambers. Another curtain could be pulled across the front. Leila could see that somebody could have been waiting in the next door change room and literally lifted up the dividing curtain and seized Sarah-Jane. The outfit she had been going to try on had been left inside, on the floor.

Strudworth came over to Charlotte. 'The abductor either came in from the back door that leads out to the lane or slipped past the salesgirl without her noticing.'

Leila had already figured as much.

'The back door wasn't locked?' asked Charlotte.

'It was but it was easy to unlock it from the inside.

Is Leila picking up anything, do you think?'

Leila wouldn't mind picking up a nice little diamond stud for her ear but not for the thousand bucks they were asking.

'I'm not sure,' said Charlotte. 'Let's have a look at the door.'

Leila had to inhale to squeeze through the narrow passageway that led past a small kitchen area to the back door, which led onto an alleyway.

'The police think the abductor had a van waiting out here.'

Strudworth gestured to the narrow alley. Charlotte led Leila down the alley.

'Back in a minute.'

'Where are we going?' asked Leila.

'To see where this takes us.'

The alley emerged onto another street. Charlotte cut through there and found herself at a bus stop. A girl her age was waiting there and was keen to pat Leila.

'Where does this bus go?' asked Charlotte.

'Downtown,' said the girl, stroking Leila's ear.

Charlotte thanked her and headed back.

'What's going on?' asked Leila. 'You look like you know something.'

'I don't know anything, Leila. But I do suspect.'

'Suspect what?'

But there was no time to answer for as they turned back towards the rear of the shop, Miss Strudworth was gesturing excitedly.

'The kidnapper is on the phone to Mr Gold.'

They hustled to the back door where Mr Gold had his phone switched to speaker. The detective was writing furiously.

'If you vant the girl return, you do as told.'

It was a young woman. She spoke with a thick accent that Leila had heard in several James Bond films – Russian, she believed.

Mr Gold was very anxious. 'Is Sarah-Jane all right?'

'I know you have police with you, don't play me for fool. One million dollar in unmarked bills. You have hours twenty plus four only. We will give further instructions. You want proof we are real deal, check change room. Red mark on wall match red mark on outfit left.'

The call rang off. The detective shook his head. 'Not long enough for a trace.'

The uniformed policeman appeared from the shop. 'The marks are there. That was the kidnapper all right. Only they would know about the red marks.'

The detective muttered bitterly. 'I'm afraid this has the hallmark of Russian mafia.'

Mr Gold could see it all. 'It was probably the woman who abducted Sarah-Jane. Waited in the neighbouring change room with chloroform or something to knock her out. Then let in help to carry her out to a waiting van.'

'My thoughts exactly,' said the detective. 'Very nasty people, these types. I hope you can get a million dollars, Mr Gold. Otherwise . . .'

He let the sentence hang ominously.

ͻ ͻ ͻ ͻ

Feathers had been brought up to speed by Leila and Charlotte, who were back in the trailer. Mr Gold had got it re-towed to his house for the time being. Feathers pushed his beak forward in thought. 'I wonder if the Russian mafia snatched the tabby as well?'

'Why didn't they ask for a ransom?' asked Leila.

'I don't know. What do you think, Charlie?'

Charlie had been sitting quietly all the way back in the car and was looking thoughtful. 'I think it's highly suspicious.'

Leila snorted. 'Of course it's suspicious, the Russian mafia is involved.'

'Are they?' asked Charlotte.

'That's what the cop said.'

'Cops know nothing,' said Feathers definitely.

'That voice on the phone, I've heard it before,' said Charlotte.

'Where? We could get a reward.'

It was the first time Leila had shown much interest in saving Sarah-Jane. She was thinking that with her cut of a reward, the diamond stud could be hers after all.

Charlotte frowned in concentration. 'I can't place it, I've heard it recently.'

'Oh my God.' Leila threw a quick look around. 'Is our door locked? It could be somebody here and if it's somebody here, who's the next target, hey? Who is the only target likely to bring in more ransom than Sarah-Jane?'

Feathers thought hard. 'Mr Gold?'

'Not Mr Gold. Me, you idiot! Charlotte, lock the trailer. I'd do it myself but my hooves aren't good with fine motor movement.'

'Do as she says, Charlie,' Feathers was peering out the curtain. 'These Russians could be lurking and I'm the prime target, not her.'

'You?'

'Who do you think Mr Gold cares about more?'

'I know who Mr Gold cares about more. His movie star!'

'Who he left in Australia!'

'Only because I bit him!'

Charlotte intervened. 'Stop it, you two. I'm not sure there is any Russian mafia.'

Leila shook her head. The kid knew nothing. 'Don't you watch *Law and Order*? The Russian mafia is always doing something bad.'

'I mean, I don't think they were involved.'

Feathers and Leila looked at each other meaningfully. Feathers used his wing to circle his ear as if to say 'crazy'.

Leila said, 'You been eating the loco weed, Charlie?'

Charlotte gave her a thin smile.

'This morning I wound up with Sarah-Jane's sports bag by mistake. It looks exactly the same as mine. Inside were a pair of pyjamas and a toiletry bag.'

Feathers and Leila looked at each other and shrugged as if to say, so?

Charlotte groaned. 'Doesn't that strike you as odd?'

Feathers shook his head. 'If *I* had a bag with pyjamas, that might be odd.'

Charlotte sighed and patiently explained. 'Sarah-Jane had a trailer here. Why wouldn't she just leave her pyjamas and toiletries in the trailer?'

'Ah,' Leila nodded smugly. 'I got it. You're right. She suspected the Russian mafia would steal them from her trailer. She was onto them!'

'NO!' Charlotte exploded in frustration.

'No?' Leila was certain she'd worked out what Charlotte was driving at.

'No. She didn't need to take pyjamas with her. And she had the bag at the boutique as well. I don't think she was kidnapped. I think she staged it, went out the back door, down the alley and jumped on a bus downtown. From there, she could have gone anywhere.'

It hit Leila with the force of a cold slab of steak right across the face. 'Of course! I thought she took my opening triumph too easily. This is all about her getting press. You're a genius, Charlie!'

Feathers was more sceptical. 'Maybe there is some other explanation . . .'

'Noooo,' whinnied Leila, 'and I know where I've heard that Russian woman. That's the exact same accent Sarah-Jane used in *Thrills and Spills*.'

Charlotte was excited. 'Yes! That's where I heard it. At the Excelsior exhibit. Do you think we should tell Mr Gold our suspicions?'

Leila was dubious. 'You'd have to be the one who told him.'

'Did anybody else see what was in the bag?' asked Feathers.

Charlotte wasn't sure.

Leila worked through it. 'So it's only your word.'

'What about the Russian voice? Can't they do some fancy scientific test to prove it was Sarah-Jane?' asked Feathers.

Leila answered. 'Suppose they do and they show it is her. What does that prove? The kidnappers could have forced her to say that. No, we don't have enough to go on. Charlie could look like she's got something against Sarah-Jane, next thing you know, she's prime suspect.'

Charlotte did not like the sound of that. 'So what can we do?'

Leila thought it was pretty obvious. 'We have to figure out where she's hiding and try to expose her before the ransom pick-up.'

'She won't be at home,' said Feathers.

'What was in the bag, Charlotte? Do you remember anything that might help us find her?'

Charlotte thought back. 'There was a folded map.'

Leila got in close, extremely animated. 'What map? Where? Think, Charlotte. Think, this is important!'

Feathers flapped a wing in recognition. 'Harrison Ford in *Witness*.'

Leila winked. 'You got it.'

Charlotte closed her eyes and tried to remember any names on the map. Letters spun around in a jumble before reassembling . . . *azquez*? She opened her eyes.

'A-z-q-u-e-z,' she said. 'I'm certain that was one word.'

'Azquez?' Feathers shook his head, at a loss.

'Was that the whole word or part of it?'

'It was all I could see.'

'But the map was folded, right? So it could be Azquez – something or something – azquez.'

'Sounds Spanish,' said Feathers, 'but there's about ten thousand Spanish place names in California.'

Charlotte suggested they get a map of California and begin looking for a match. 'Maybe then I'll recognise the rest of the area?'

Leila said, 'California is a big place. I don't think Sarah-Jane would be taking herself too far. She can't drive and she wouldn't want anybody in on it. She'd go by bus or train. Let's look for a two-hundred-mile radius from L.A.'

Feathers said, 'Mr Gold has a big library. Come on, Charlotte.'

Charlotte and Feathers left Leila watching news footage of herself arriving at the Melrose boutique. The press still didn't know what was going on and the police and studio were laying a false trail, hinting that it was actually a scene from the upcoming movie. On the way to the library Charlotte passed Hector

Martinez, Mr Gold and Hawthorn in a low and troubled conversation.

'Anything happens to her, we're dead in the water,' said Martinez gravely.

'Straight to the bottom,' offered Hawthorn.

'You don't need to tell me,' said Mr Gold.

Charlotte felt very sorry for him. He was a nice man and this movie had been a horror for him. The library was indeed enormous and it was just as well she had Feathers with her because the maps were high up and Feathers was more quickly able to locate what they needed. Charlotte had to climb a library ladder to fetch them.

Back in the trailer they spread out a detailed map of California and took sections, looking for any town with the letters *azquez*. It was about fifteen minutes later when Charlotte spotted something.

'Look here. Valazquez Ravine.'

Leila and Feathers crowded in to check out the area, which was about one hundred miles north-east of Los Angeles.

'I know that area!' Leila was excited. 'We shot some scenes near there during *Horses for Courses*, in an old, disused mining town. 'It was right . . . here.'

She put her hoof on the map but it covered about twenty square miles.

'Move your big fat hoof, I can't see,' whined Feathers.

'How would you like my big fat hoof on your tiny bird brain?'

Charlotte, again, had to arbitrate. 'Guys, cut it out. Leila, let us see, please.'

Leila removed her hoof. 'See, just there, Gilbertsville. There's nobody around for miles. A coach runs from the city.'

'There's only one problem,' observed Feathers. 'The hundred miles between here and there. How are we going to get there?'

Charlotte said, 'Obviously I can't drive . . .'

She looked at Leila. 'Oh no. No way I'm walking there. And don't even think about suggesting the coach.'

'I know!' said Charlotte. 'I can ask Strudworth to drive us.'

'You going to tell her what we think?' Feathers sounded doubtful.

Charlotte said, 'She's a good person. I think we can trust her.'

ↄ ↄ ↄ

Charlotte found Strudworth in her bungalow, pacing about, concerned.

'It's awful, Charlotte. I really feel I should be doing something to help Joel.'

'Well –' Charlotte took the plunge – 'that's kind of why I'm here.'

Strudworth regarded her. Her eyebrow raised in a question. 'Go on.'

Charlotte told her everything. Strudworth listened without interrupting.

'You feel that if you go to the police, you'll be suspected of creating mischief or being a loony? Hmm. Believe me, I know the feeling.' Strudworth was conducting some inner struggle. 'The thing is, I feel very uncomfortable deceiving Mr Gold.'

'If we tell Mr Gold, he will have to tell the police.'

Strudworth nodded. 'Yes. If we're right, Sarah-Jane could be charged by the police, which will not help the movie. And if we're wrong and something terrible were to happen . . .'

Strudworth's head shot upwards. She had made her decision. 'Very well, we leave at dawn.'

'Apparently, it's very difficult terrain. We should take Leila. Give her some exercise anyway.'

'Good idea.'

The phone buzzed and Strudworth seized it swiftly.

'Yes?' There was a pause. Her eyes fell on Charlotte. 'Yes, she is.' She held the phone out. 'It's Todd Greycroft.'

Charlotte took the call. 'Hi, Todd. I'm so sorry, things have been hectic here and I have no idea how you did?'

'Came fourth.'

Charlotte thought that was excellent, given the experience of the other riders.

'So now I'm all finished. I'm coming up to L.A. tomorrow.'

Charlotte thought quickly. 'Can you bring Warrior?'

'I suppose. Why?'

'I'll tell you tomorrow. We might have to camp out for a night though.'

'Sounds very mysterious.'

Charlotte gave him Mr Gold's address.

'I can be there by 8 am,' said Todd.

Charlotte rang off, feeling excited and relieved. Todd had a very cool head in a crisis. She knew she could trust him to help.

'I gather he's joining us,' said Strudworth.

Charlotte realised she hadn't even asked Strudworth. 'Is that okay?'

'I'm sure he'll be an asset. I'll organise the horse floats. Now get a good night's rest.'

Charlotte wasn't sure she would be able to sleep a wink.

Chapter 11

As it turned out, Charlotte slept well. It was Leila who was antsy. The next morning she was in a panic, trying to look her best.

'Try the pink bridle,' she commanded Charlotte, who was walking around in one boot, looking to get the other one on.

'Give me a break, I'm not dressed myself.'

'Like anyone would notice. Come on, hop to it.'

Charlotte found the pink bridle and slipped it on Leila, who regarded herself in the mirror.

'Is it too evening with the pink? Try the rhinestone one.'

'I haven't got . . .'

'Rhinestone. Come on, make it snappy.'

Charlotte kept her cool, and tried the rhinestone bridle on Leila, who peered at herself in the giant mirror.

She shook her head. 'Nope, that is definitely too evening. What about the western-style?'

Charlotte threw that on her.

'Maybe too try-hard,' observed Leila, checking herself from every possible angle.

Charlotte had had enough. 'You're wearing this.'

She slipped on Leila's normal work bridle.

'But it's so plain!' whined Leila.

'It will make your eyes stand out better,' offered Charlotte, giving herself time to pull on her other boot.

'Maybe you're right.' Leila tilted her head around, satisfied. 'Okay, now my mane. I'd like a little French braid.'

'You told me never to plait your mane!'

Charlotte was throwing clothes into her backpack. Feathers was still snoozing on his perch.

Leila said, 'You know better than to listen to me.'

There was a rap on the door.

'Charlotte. Are you ready?' It was Strudworth.

'Not quite.' Charlotte desperately seized clothes and threw them into the bag.

'We need to get an early start. The traffic out of the city will be horrendous.'

Leila had momentarily forgotten how bad it could be stuck in a horse float on an L.A. freeway. At least it would leave some jaw-time with Warrior. But then Warrior could be precious. If he was in one of his moods it would be like going to the dentist. She would need a distraction. She nudged Charlotte.

'You better pack my iHorse too. The one marked Nashville. Seeing as we're heading to the Wild West, I think country – Keith Urban and Travis Tritt.'

'Is there somebody in there with you?' asked Strudworth suspiciously.

'It's the TV.'

Charlotte glared at Leila, grabbed the map, stuck it in her pocket and opened the door to find Miss Strudworth on the step, in very neat tweed.

'Let's go, Richards. Todd Greycroft has just arrived.'

Charlotte and Leila needed no incentive to leave the trailer. Feathers remained drooped on his perch, snoozing.

Todd and Warrior were waiting in the driveway. Todd, in jeans and a denim shirt, looked ready for a trail ride. Leila left the humans to jabber among themselves and sauntered up to Warrior. She decided to get the first shot across his bow.

'Only fourth?' she said in Horswegian.

Warrior looked at her with his piercing brown eyes. 'Not bad out of fifty-four.'

'I hear dressage was your weakness again.' She enjoyed needling him.

Warrior grunted. 'It's such a girly thing. All that prancing and dancing.'

'In other words you suck royally at it.'

'Like you do at the jumps.'

'Hey, I started late.'

'Any time you need a little schooling . . .' Warrior shrugged.

Leila wouldn't mind a little schooling with the black stallion but no way would she admit that to the arrogant fathead! She changed the subject. 'You want me to fill you in on what this is about?'

'Fire away.'

'Believe me, I can take my time. We've got a long road trip ahead of us.'

Leila noticed Charlotte and Todd heading for them.

'I like your bridle,' said Warrior.

'You do?'

'Yeah. I figured you'd be wearing hot pink or some kind of bling. That looks more natural.'

Leila felt a little tingle down her spine. She loved it when Warrior gave her a compliment.

The traffic was every bit as bad as they had imagined, but with Todd for company, Charlotte hardly cared.

Miss Strudworth found a station playing classical music and settled back while Charlotte told Todd all that had happened – well, not quite all – she had to be inventive now and again to keep Leila out of it.

'So how did you know that they filmed part of the movie in this old mining town?' asked Todd innocently.

'Yes,' echoed Strudworth. 'I meant to ask the same thing.'

Charlotte's brain rattled quickly. 'I think Honey Grace mentioned it at some point.'

Oh no, there it was again – another Hollywood lie. Charlotte was reminded of poor Honey's problems. Since this Sarah-Jane business she'd forgotten all about Oscar.

They cleared one freeway and got onto another where the traffic moved much more freely.

'So what's the plan?' asked Todd.

'I'm afraid I haven't really thought of one other than we get to this place and see if Sarah-Jane is hiding out there.'

'She could have moved on.'

'Yes, she could have,' Charlotte was forced to admit.

'What about this million dollars the kidnapper – Sarah-Jane or whoever – demanded?' asked Todd.

Strudworth revealed the studio was getting it together.

'But is Sarah-Jane planning to pick up the money?' asked Todd.

'I doubt it,' said Charlotte. 'I think she'll turn up and say that she escaped. Then she'll be front-page news and a hero, which is what she wants.'

'You could just wait, then,' suggested Todd. 'Not bother to look for her at all.'

It was Strudworth who answered. 'And let her get away with putting Mr Gold through all this? No. She needs to be taught a lesson.'

In the float, Leila had run through much the same for Warrior. He commented that he couldn't see why anybody cared what happened to some selfish actor. Leila wasn't sure if he was talking about the particular case of Sarah-Jane or whether he was lumping all actors into that category.

'Actors are no worse than show-jumpers,' she said.

He made some grunt from deep in his chest and said, 'So I suppose you've been out partying every night?'

Leila hated that superior tone he adopted.

'Do you know anything about the movie industry?'

'You get paid a lot of money for pulling faces,' he said.

'That's what you think? You have no idea. As a matter of fact I've been training hard.' She told him about the run-in with the mountain lion, swapping her role and Charlotte's of course to make herself sound like the hero, which in fact she'd actually convinced herself of. She also told him about the narrow escape at Excelsior Studios. He listened with interest.

'And I suppose you've caught up with a few old boyfriends?'

He asked it casually but Leila was able to sift through the smoke. She was ecstatic! Warrior was jealous. And if he was jealous, that meant he cared. And if he cared . . . Hmm, how to play this?

'I bumped into one or two old running mates,' she lied with a hint of evasion. 'I suppose you were busy showing off your muscles to some little Argentine filly down there in San Diego.'

'Actually, they stabled us next to the Germans. I'll say one thing about those German mares, they sure can dance.'

Huh. Leila found herself getting prickly all over. If those little Fräuleins came anywhere near Warrior when she was around, they'd wind up with size 10 Ferragamo shoeprints all over their foreheads.

Todd was navigating. It reminded Charlotte of her father, who would let her hold the map, ask her the direction they needed to take but still have to check it for himself. It didn't really bother Charlotte though as map reading wasn't her greatest skill. She was much better out in the open following a trail that would be invisible to ninety-nine per cent of people. Jimmy Possum, one of the Aboriginal stockmen, had taught her tracking skills. They had been in the car for something like three hours when Strudworth spied the little sign to Gilbertsville. Another ten minutes and the dirt road ran out. Strudworth pulled over and they all climbed out of the car. The day was cooking hot, the sky blue, the earth crisp. They had not seen a person or vehicle since turning off the freeway. They advanced a few hundred metres to the edge of a ridge. In the valley below, some rusting buildings were visible.

'I guess that's it,' said Todd.

It didn't appear to be too long a walk. Maybe twenty to thirty minutes. They unloaded Leila and Warrior, locked up the car and started off. The terrain was not dissimilar to Snake Hills – a lot of sand and rock dotted with scrubby vegetation.

'Somebody has walked through here recently,' said Charlotte, pointing at the soft sand.

'You can tell that?' Strudworth was dubious.

Charlotte pointed out some tiny flattened plants. She could also see part footprints all the way to the bottom, which Todd could not detect at all.

'You're very cool, Charlotte,' he said, impressed.

The path down was slippery and Leila and Warrior had to pick their way carefully, which meant it took them a little longer than anticipated to reach the bottom. Leila recalled the spot well. Tommy had done some very fine close-ups under the large cacti and the chef had served up a magnificent crab salad. Leila had also hidden some cacti in Sarah-Jane's face flannel and when she went to remove her make-up . . . Ah, Leila chuckled at the memory.

Charlotte diverted slightly from the course and bent down to pick something up. She returned and showed the others a very recently discarded empty plastic soda bottle.

'It's the brand Sarah-Jane drinks,' said Charlotte. She was glad she wasn't alone here. This place was eerie. The buildings that had once been a bustling gold town were falling apart. The timber had rotted away in places, leaving gaping holes. The tin roofs had rusted and fallen in. The wind keened through what was left of the structures. Charlotte recognised a narrow twisting shape in the sand.

'Snakes.'

'Not the kind of place I would choose to stay,' said Strudworth.

'Though I suppose you're not likely to get visitors,' offered Todd.

Leila had a fair idea where Sarah-Jane would be holed up. At the other end of the town was what had once been the saloon. It was the most intact structure. She let out a whinny and began trotting in that direction.

'Looks like Leila might have picked up her scent,' observed Strudworth.

Charlotte knew the only way Leila would have picked up her scent would be if Sarah-Jane had rolled herself in pizza, but she played along. The others followed and came to the saloon. It had no front door but, amazingly, the high roof was still largely intact, as were most of the wooden walls. Todd didn't hesitate, he strode in. Charlotte and Strudworth followed. They emerged into a large open room which one could imagine might have been impressive in its day. Little of the wooden floor remained. The planks had been torn up and probably used for fires to keep campers warm at night. Charlotte knew from her own experience that deserts could get very cold once the sun dropped. With the wind howling, it would be quite scary. For the first time she wondered if Sarah-Jane really would go through all that for the publicity.

'Here,' called Strudworth from around the other side of an alcove. Charlotte rounded it to find her holding up the sports bag.

Apparently Sarah-Jane would endure quite a bit for publicity. There was no sign of Sarah-Jane but an expensive sleeping bag had been laid out ready for sleep with a camping light, a bag full of food, bottles of water and the pyjamas Charlotte had seen.

'Maybe she has gone to pick up the ransom,' said Todd.

Charlotte, however, didn't think that. 'Something's wrong.'

'What do you mean?' asked Strudworth.

Charlotte pointed. 'The sleeping bag wasn't slept in and the pyjamas haven't been used.'

The others could see she was right.

'Maybe she went to stage her kidnap and now she has been kidnapped for real?' speculated Strudworth.

'Try your phone, Todd,' suggested Charlotte, giving him Mr Gold's number.

He tried but there was no signal. They took themselves outside but it didn't help.

'You probably have to get up to the top of the ridge,' said Todd.

'If she made that call pretending to be the Russian woman from up there last night, she would have had to find her way back in the dark. She could have got lost,' said Charlotte.

'Sarah-Jane! Are you here?' yelled Strudworth in her loud voice. Nothing. Strudworth suggested they cover the town first. Charlotte mounted Leila and Todd mounted Warrior. Strudworth searched by foot.

It took less than fifteen minutes to cover the old township but there was no sign of her. They regrouped in what had once been the town square.

Charlotte looked around them. It was possible that even where they had left the car the higher mountains behind might block any phone signal. So if Sarah-Jane had gone to make a call, she might have had to venture further up.

'It looks like rough country. She could easily have slipped and hurt herself,' said Todd.

Strudworth thought she should try to contact Mr Gold to get help searching.

'It's clear she was here,' she pointed out.

Charlotte agreed that was the best plan but in the meantime, she thought she and Todd should start looking. But where? Charlotte slowly circled the perimeter of the town on Leila and this time she found indications that Sarah-Jane had headed south. Unfortunately the track quickly ran out.

'I don't like the look of that.'

Charlotte was staring at the ground. Leila couldn't see what she was talking about.

'What's "that"?'

'A pack of coyotes.'

'Here we go again,' said Leila.

'Come on,' said Charlotte, 'you scared off the mountain lion, didn't you?'

Leila hated it when Charlotte outsmarted her. They returned to Todd and Miss Strudworth and determined she would head back to the car. If she could get no signal using the mobile phone she would drive to the freeway and find a phone box or gas station. In the meantime Todd and Warrior would take the eastern end of the range and Charlotte and Leila the west.

'What do we do if we find her and she's hurt?'

Todd's question was a good one. They couldn't leave her and they had no means of communication other than their voices.

'Let's meet back in two hours time. If one of us isn't here it means they've found her and the other will go to help.'

That seemed like a plan. Charlotte knew from growing up in the Australian outback that the most important thing for survival was water. You could survive without food for days, but not without water, and already the valley was like a furnace. They made sure they had plenty of bottles. Leila rubbed up close to Warrior.

'Bet we find her before you,' she whinnied.

'What are we playing for?'

'You lose, you have to do a slow waltz with me in the dressage ring.'

Warrior let out a low groan. 'And if you lose?'

'I have to do a slow waltz with you in the dressage ring,' she chuckled.

'Ha ha. You lose, you have to massage my back.'

Hmm, thought Leila, not that bad an option. Either way, she and Warrior were getting up close and personal. 'Deal.'

They began slowly working out in a zigzag pattern. Charlotte studied the ground, carefully looking for footprints, but she figured the wind had probably wiped them away. Every now and again she found more coyote prints. She was also looking at the low scrub for any sign that the foliage had been trampled or broken. Nothing all the way to where the ground started to rise again on the far hillside, probably three kilometres from the old town. She used her knees to urge Leila up the slippery slope.

'Do we really have to?' whined Leila. 'Last thing I need is a broken leg.'

'You can do it,' said Charlotte reassuringly.

Leila slowly picked her way up the hill. More than once she asked herself why she was doing this for that brat anyway. Couldn't they just cast somebody else? As soon as she thought that, Leila felt bad. True, Sarah-Jane was a pain but Leila didn't want her to be badly hurt.

After another twenty minutes of fruitless searching Charlotte eased up and looked around her. Nothing. She could just spy Todd, a dot on the far ridge, moving slowly.

'Coo-ee,' she hollered and listened to her voice bounce around the canyon.

'Coo-ee,' came the faint reply.

'You wearing that Sarah-Jane perfume by any chance?' asked Leila. Her nostrils had picked up the faintest tang.

'No. I'm saving my bottle as a present for Hannah.'

'Well, somebody is.'

'You sure?'

'Charlie, I spent half my Hollywood life smelling expensive perfume so I know a cheap one when I sniff it.'

Charlotte was excited. She swivelled in the saddle, feeling the direction of the wind against her face.

'This way.' She turned Leila into the breeze, which had freshened, no doubt the reason Leila had been able to smell the perfume. The tell-tale glint of sun on glass flicked off the ground, only for an instant but for Charlotte it was enough. She galloped Leila the two hundred metres towards it and dismounted.

Sure enough, here was one of the perfume bottles that had been supplied in the gift bags. The bottle had fallen but not broken and the perfume leaked very slowly from the top. Charlotte thought the most likely explanation was that Sarah-Jane had lost it from her bag, maybe while taking out or replacing her phone.

'Sarah-Jane?' she yelled loudly.

The only reply was whistling wind.

'Sarah-Jane?' she yelled again.

Still no answer.

She examined the area carefully and about five metres on found a sagebrush that had been flattened. Now she was growing excited.

'So she came this way?' asked Leila.

'I'm pretty certain. Coo-eee,' she called as loudly as she could but there was no reply and she could no longer see Todd on the far ridge. 'You search over there,' she pointed, 'I'll search over here. Call out if you see anything like a footprint, a flattened bush –'

'– or a candy wrapper?' asked Leila.

'Do you see a candy wrapper?' Charlotte could barely contain her excitement.

'No, but that's the kind of thing I'm looking for, right?'

'Yes, Leila. That's the kind of thing.'

'And could you put my iHorse on? It's kind of boring out here.'

Charlotte pulled the small player and earphones from her bag and pushed them into Leila's ears.

Leila smiled at the sound of that country twang. 'Sweet.'

She started off, humming horribly out of tune. Charlotte tried to ignore her and began slowly walking, scrutinising every centimetre of the hard earth in a long sweep. Nothing. Nothing. Nothing.

She stopped suddenly. Had she heard something? Her first thought was leakage from Leila's iHorse, but Leila was too far away. No, there it was again. Charlotte took another step forward ...

The ground beneath her feet collapsed without warning. So shocked was she that she barely had time to squeal. All she knew was she was falling into a deep black pit.

Chapter 12

The few seconds it took Charlotte to fall seemed more like a few minutes. It was the weirdest sensation, like falling off a horse from the top of the highest steeple. The sunlight above was swallowed by black as she plunged. She braced for the impact she hoped would come sooner rather than later because she knew with each passing second the landing would be harder.

Thump.

Whatever she landed on was softer than she had anticipated. Almost like feathers. She lay on her back, breathing for a long moment, running through a checklist. She was thinking clearly. No concussion. Good. Arms and leds could move. She didn't feel any pain so hopefully no bones had been broken. She struggled up. It was very dark down here but as her eyes grew accustomed to it she realised that she had fallen into a mound of fine soft dirt. Further investigation allowed her to see she was in some kind of earthen tunnel. Okay, this had been a gold town, chances were this was some old mine shaft. She manoeuvred herself below the hole where she had fallen. It seemed to be about three metres above her. No way to climb up. She yelled.

'Leila!'

ꚉ ꚉ ꚉ ꚉ

Leila was grooving to some Randy Travis. That boy had a voice on him as sweet as molasses. She swayed this way and that. The sun was a little too hot for her liking but other than that it was quite pleasant. She looked back to ask Charlotte if she had any treats on her but there was no Charlotte. She had been there a minute ago. Where on earth was she?

ꚉ ꚉ ꚉ ꚉ

'Leila!'

Charlotte grunted in frustration. That darn iHorse! Leila couldn't hear her.

'Help.'

The voice came from somewhere back there in the dark. It was very faint but Charlotte knew that she had definitely heard it.

'Sarah-Jane?' she called.

For a long moment there was no reply and Charlotte was tempted to think she had imagined it after all. Then came a weak plea.

'Help me.'

Charlotte tiptoed into the dark musty heart of the tunnel. It was pitch black down here. Some light flickered to her left and she changed direction, feeling her way along the earthen walls. It seemed that the tunnel was quite broad, easily wide enough for her to walk with her arms spread and her fingers touching each side. The light went out, then flicked back on.

'Sarah-Jane?'

'Down here,' came the anxious voice. Not at all like the bossy Sarah-Jane Charlotte was used to. Now Charlotte could see her. Or the top half of her at least. The rest was covered by a thick mound of earth.

'What happened?' asked Charlotte, who saw the light was from Sarah-Jane's mobile phone.

'The earth collapsed and fell in on top of me. I can't move my legs . . .' Sarah-Jane turned the phone towards Charlotte, illuminating her face. 'You?' She sounded extremely disappointed.

'The name's Charlotte.'

'This is all your fault.'

Charlotte was taken aback. She was about to ask

how it was her fault but Sarah-Jane saved her the trouble.

'You turn up here as Leila's new best pal and suddenly all the attention is on you. Just because you throw a few snakes around you think you're a star.'

Charlotte had heard enough.

'For a start, I have no intention of being a star. I simply came to help out Miss Strudworth and Leila. And, secondly, if I'm that much of a problem I'll leave somebody else to rescue you.'

Charlotte turned on her heel.

'No, please, I'm sorry. Okay? Don't leave me. Please get me out. I'll give you my Palm pilot, my Blackberry, anything.'

Charlotte turned back and sighed. 'You don't get it.'

'Fine. You want my motorised scooter . . .'

'I don't want anything from you except for you to finish the movie and stop fighting with Leila.'

'Oh.' Sarah-Jane was shocked. 'Okay, then. You get me out of here I'll give you all that other stuff anyway. Where are the others?'

Charlotte said, 'I'm afraid I'm the only one here right now. My friend Todd is off checking the other ridge and Miss Strudworth is calling for help.'

Sarah-Jane let out a whimper. 'I've been here for

hours. I thought nobody would come. I'm dying of thirst.'

Charlotte opened the bottle she had slung over her shoulder and passed it to Sarah-Jane, who guzzled greedily for a long moment.

'Oh, thank you,' she gasped and wiped her mouth. 'How are you going to get me out?'

'I'm not sure.' Charlotte explained that she had fallen through the earth as well.

'You mean we're both trapped?' Sarah-Jane almost screamed it.

Thinking negatively was not something Charlotte was accustomed to. 'People will find us.'

'Yes, but when? The earth here is shifting all the time. The whole thing could come down on us.'

'Let's see if I can dig you out.'

'I think there's some old wooden beam or something across my foot.'

Charlotte began digging away.

'Was it cold down here last night?'

'No, it wasn't too bad. But I was so scared no-one would ever find me. In fact, how *did* you find me?'

Charlotte ran through the series of events which had led her here, leaving out Leila as the informant.

'You're right,' admitted Sarah-Jane. 'I was very stupid. I was just annoyed Leila was getting all the publicity. I mean, you probably think I'm exaggerating but it's almost like she's human.'

'I know what you mean.'

Charlotte had dug out enough of the earth to find Sarah-Jane's foot.

'Can you feel that?' She squeezed through Sarah-Jane's boot.

'Yes.'

'That's good. I don't think there's any major damage.' Charlotte kept digging, finally revealing the beam, which was very thick. 'I think this will be too heavy for me to lift by myself. I better go back to where I fell and see if Leila is waiting.'

'Don't leave me, please.'

'I have to if you're going to get out of this.'

Charlotte edged her way back along the tunnel walls. As she did she was acutely aware of the sound of falling sand. Not a lot, but it seemed constant. Sarah-Jane had been right about one thing. This whole tunnel could cave in at any time. She found her way back to the area where she had fallen and saw she had been lucky that some timber supports were placed right here on either side. While the roof had caved in when she'd walked on it, the damage had been limited by the structural support on the sides.

'Leila,' she yelled up. 'Where are you?'

Up above, Leila was perplexed. Where had Charlotte gone? It was relatively flat terrain here and very sparse. No big boulders or trees for her to be concealed behind. Leila's earpiece wire got hooked up on a small piece of foliage and as she turned to scan the landscape, her earpiece was yanked out. Great. Try getting those back in with hooves!

'Leila, I need you.'

Charlotte's voice. Leila looked around. Was she imagining it?

'Leila! I've got pizza.'

Pizza? Yum. How did Charlotte find pizza out here? Leila trotted in the direction of the voice.

'Charlie, you're a gem. What kind of . . .'

'Leila. Stop.'

Leila stopped confused. Where was Charlotte?

'You got me on CCTV or something?'

'I'm in a mine shaft. The ground gave way. Sarah-Jane's trapped too. Be very careful, the earth is crumbling.'

Leila edged slowly forward.

'Sarah-Jane's got the pizza?'

'No. I just said that to get your attention! I'm

about two metres down. I need you to bring Todd back here, with a rope. Sarah-Jane is trapped under a beam.'

'How am I going to get a rope?'

'I don't know. You'll figure something out. And hurry. I'm not sure how long this tunnel will hold.'

Leila edged right to the lip of the hole in the ground. She craned her neck full stretch and could just see Charlotte. She really was trapped.

'Come on, Leila. Don't let me down.'

'You know me, Charlie. Leila comes through.'

Charlotte's heart sank as she heard Leila gallop off. She hoped this would not be the last time she would ever hear that sound.

ᴐ ᴐ ᴐ ᴐ

Leila galloped with all her might. Every second was precious. She had to head back down the slope, which was treacherous, offering little support. If she snapped a leg, that was it – for her and Charlotte. But there was no time to worry about that. Leila skidded down at an angle, feeling flesh rip on the rocks. Consuela would have her hands full dealing with that! Leila levelled off and began charging around a narrow pass that would bring her back above the old town, about the level of where they had originally parked. She rounded a corner and hit the skids.

Blocking her way was a pack of mean, hungry coyotes. Instinctively, she thought about backing up but the low growls coming from behind told her more were there. And then she spied a couple above her, spittle around their hungry mouths. She wasn't sure she could take the ones in front at a charge because the pass was narrow. Even if she skittled a few, the others would rip into her.

Which left only one option. Down.

She began galloping at the coyotes in front. They didn't budge. Their lean, muscular bodies tensed to spring. She sprang first, leaping out into thin air. She felt herself falling. There was nowhere soft to aim for a landing, so she tucked in her legs and offered her rump.

YOW!!!

It was, she imagined, like being hit in the backside by shot pellets. She skidded down the slope, a little like the time she'd been tobogganing in Vail except without the toboggan. She hit the valley floor and regained her feet. Her rump was stinging but she ignored it and charged into the old township. Looking up, she could just see Warrior on the opposite ridge to where she had been. She reared on her hind legs and whinnied louder than she had ever whinnied before.

♫ ♫ ♫

'Is somebody coming?' asked a fretful Sarah-Jane.

Charlotte continued to dig around Sarah-Jane's trapped leg. Sarah-Jane did what she could to contribute.

'I hope so. I asked Leila to go find my friend.'

'Leila? All she'll find is a stylist.'

'I don't think you know the real Leila,' said Charlotte. There was a long pause as Charlotte concentrated on digging and tried not to think whether the walls would hold. Little rivulets of sand continued to fall on them.

'I'm sorry I was rude to you before.'

Charlotte felt sorry for Sarah-Jane. For the first time she seemed human.

'Believe me, I don't want to be a star,' said Charlotte.

'I feel like that a lot myself,' said Sarah-Jane. 'I don't have any real friends in Los Angeles.'

'Can't you make any?'

'You don't understand. It's not the same. All the kids I meet my age just want to be me. Or worse, replace me. I hardly even get to ride any more because I'm always doing interviews or home schooling or being fitted for wardrobe.'

Charlotte had, by now, dug all around Sarah-Jane's boots and along more of the fallen beam trapping her.

'Can you pull your legs back out?'

Sarah-Jane grimaced and gave it her all, but to no avail.

'I'm wedged too tight.'

Charlotte tried to lift the beam but there was still a lot of earth on it. Unfortunately, all she succeeded in doing was increasing the flow of dirt from above.

Sarah-Jane wailed. 'I'm going to die. I'm never going to get out of here.'

And then she began crying steadily.

∩ ∩ ∩ ∩

Warrior was moving carefully over the ground as Todd's boots were commanding him. He enjoyed the to and fro with Leila. She was a challenge, that was for sure. He stopped in his tracks. His name was being called. In horse. By Leila. He looked down from the ridge, back to the old ghost town and far below saw the amazing sight of Leila rearing on her hind legs and pumping her forelegs.

No Charlotte. Something was wrong. He needed to make sure Todd got it. Warrior began snorting and circling.

Alerted by Warrior's behaviour, Todd broke off from his search.

'What's up, fella?'

Warrior was jerking his head down. Todd had not heard Leila but he could certainly see her. Like Warrior he realised instantly that there was no Charlotte and something was amiss.

'Come on.'

He didn't have to urge Warrior, the big stallion was already powering down the slippery ridge.

ↄ ↄ ↄ ↄ

Leila's heart beat fast at the sight of that magnificent stallion risking his life to heed her call. His balance was amazing. Somehow he almost side-gaited down the ridge, hit the bottom at pace and came powering towards her. Leila didn't wait to exchange niceties, she turned tail and galloped back knowing Warrior and Todd would follow. Getting up the slope she had just come down was no walk in the park. Her rump was still hurting and she knew she had skinned her legs but she pushed upwards. The coyotes were still there, peering down at her, but when they saw Warrior and Todd they melted back into the canyon. Leila felt the breeze tearing at her face as she galloped at maximum speed. Despite the thunder of her own hooves she could hear the echo of Warrior's. She rounded the narrow pass and ran up to the plateau area where the mine shaft was. As she neared the spot where the ground had given way, she stopped and let out a loud yell. 'Charlotte!'

Warrior thundered in not far behind her and stopped.

Todd dismounted. He could have sworn he had heard a woman call Charlotte's name. It hadn't sounded like Strudworth and there was no sign of anybody except Leila. Weird – but right now he needed to find her. Leila had clearly come for help. It was his turn to yell.

'Charlotte?'

He started towards the hole. Leila fired a warning to Warrior: 'Stop him. There's a cave-in.'

Warrior shifted to block his path.

'What is it, guys? What are you trying to tell me?'

Leila sighed. Her secret, that she could talk human, had been hers and Charlotte's alone but now she was going to have to give it up. So be it. Charlotte's life was at stake and if it meant a lifetime of electrodes clamped to her body by egghead scientists, it was the price she would have to pay. She opened her mouth to tell Todd what was happening but before she could speak, Charlotte's voice rose from the ground.

'Todd, is that you?'

'Charlotte?'

He stepped forward, trying to place the source of the sound.

Charlotte was thrilled to hear Todd's voice. She had heard Leila's yell a moment earlier and knew Leila had come through.

'Careful, Todd, the ground is very dangerous. I'm trapped in a shaft. Sarah-Jane's here. She can't move. There's a beam across her leg. Do you have a rope?'

Oops, thought Leila. She had forgotten all about that part.

'Have I got a rope?' answered Todd, his voice soaked in surprise. 'Of course I've got a rope. You said we were going camping.'

By now he had located where Charlotte's voice was coming from.

Charlotte was thinking about how heavy that beam was.

'I think you're going to need both horses to shift this beam.'

Todd moved quickly. The rope was strong nylon. He produced a sharp pocket knife and cut the rope in two. Then he tied one end around the pommel of each saddle.

'You guys are going to have to work together,' he told Warrior and Leila, before he scurried back to the hole.

'What do you think, Warrior? You up to a little working in sync?' shot Leila.

'You bet your hindquarters I am. Have you got the muscle?'

'I've got as much muscle as you. Just mine isn't all in my head,' she cracked, trying to use humour to stop herself from feeling as worried for Charlotte as she really was.

'I'm tossing the rope,' called Todd.

Two ends of rope dropped down the hole. Charlotte reached up and seized them.

'And here's my knife,' called Todd.

Charlotte moved just in time as the pocket knife plodded in the earth at her feet.

'Got it,' she called back, starting back along the tunnel.

'Hurry,' said Sarah-Jane from the dark as she heard her approach. 'The sand is falling faster all the time.'

Just as she said that another chunk fell, this time from directly above her. It smashed onto her head and broke up. Sarah-Jane didn't complain. She was too frantic, helping Charlotte dig away more dirt to expose the beam trapping her. Once both sides of the beam were exposed, Charlotte looped one rope around one end of the beam and the other around the other end of the beam. Then she tied them off with secure knots.

'Nearly there,' she assured Sarah-Jane, and charged back up the tunnel. All the activity was making things worse, bigger hunks of sand falling all the time along the entire length of the tunnel. She reached the hole.

'Okay, Todd, ready to go.'

Todd faced Leila and Warrior, who stood side by side.

'Guys, you have to do this very evenly. Understand?'

Course I understand, Todd, thought Leila. Just like applying fake tan. You had to be smooth all over.

'The earth is unstable. If we jerk this beam we might bury them,' he told them, then realised what he was doing. They were horses, they didn't know what he was saying.

But, of course, Leila did know. Thanks for upping the pressure, she thought. His shoulders against their rumps, Todd braced himself behind them, taking one rope in each hand using it as a guide to keep the rope tight.

'Go.'

Leila looked at Warrior. Warrior looked at Leila.

He offered a low whinny. 'I know,' he was saying, 'she's everything to you. Don't worry. We'll do it.'

Leila wanted to lay a big sloppy kiss on him right there.

They started forward. The rope became taut. Leila felt the weight against her. It gave her an unpleasant memory of the time she'd had to cart logs for some illegal loggers.

'Easy,' said Todd.

Leila and Warrior breathed in sync. Straining every muscle they edged forward.

ↄ ↄ ↄ ↄ

Charlotte had returned to where Sarah-Jane lay trapped. She watched as the taut ropes began to shift the beam.

'Can you move your legs?'

'I've got no circulation.'

The beam was wobbling free of the dirt. Charlotte leaned over.

'Grab my neck.'

Sarah-Jane got her arms around Charlotte's neck. Charlotte stood and pulled. Sarah-Jane's legs came free.

'Thank God,' Sarah-Jane shrieked in delight.

No sooner had Charlotte dragged her from where she had lain than a huge clump of dirt fell right where Sarah-Jane had just been.

The cave-in had started.

Chapter 13

With Sarah-Jane's arm slung around her neck, Charlotte tried to move but Sarah-Jane's legs were still numb and she could barely contribute. Charlotte more or less dragged her as the earthen roof of the tunnel collapsed behind her, each thump drawing closer to her heels. Charlotte knew she couldn't outrun it.

'Nooooo,' Sarah-Jane screamed.

In seconds they would be buried. The taut ropes were either side of them. Charlotte flipped open Todd's pocket knife.

'Come on!' screamed Sarah-Jane.

'Hold on!' yelled Charlotte, shoving one rope into Sarah-Jane's hands. She grabbed the other. As the cloud of dirt enveloped them she yelled with all her might.

'Go, Leila!'

Sand filled her lungs and began to choke her. It was

too dark to see in the core of the dust storm. She slashed blindly at the ropes and prayed.

Up above, Todd watched in horror as the ground collapsed inwards and loose sand rushed to fill up the empty space where the tunnel had been. It was like watching dominoes fall, a line racing quickly towards the hole, their only escape route. Charlotte would be buried beneath tonnes of dirt. He heard a chilling scream from below ground and then quite clearly Charlotte's yell.

Leila and Warrior felt the ropes go slack an instant before Charlotte's last desperate cry. The ropes, suddenly free of weight, gave them impetus, propelling them forward. Leila accelerated to a gallop and Warrior responded, because that was what Charlotte had commanded.

In the shaft Charlotte could not breathe. The dirt was smothering her, knocking her from her feet, almost to her waist when she felt the jerk on her arms as the rope pulled taut again. She was plucked from the swirling storm, dragged along the ground bouncing and then hoisted from her feet towards the light.

Todd couldn't believe his eyes. Head to toe in black dirt, Charlotte and Sarah-Jane burst out of the hole like fish on a line. They slithered for about ten metres before letting go and laying on their backs coughing and panting. The fault line showing the collapse continued on for another fifty metres before petering out. Todd rushed to them.

'You okay?'

'Perfect,' gasped Charlotte, reaching for his water. She rinsed out her mouth and passed the bottle to Sarah-Jane, who did the same.

Leila trotted back, shaking her mane. That dirt was going to take more than conditioner to get out. And as for the nails, maybe amputation would be necessary. Her heart was beating rapidly. Ecstatic as she was, she couldn't help but feel the shiver of how close she had come to losing Charlotte. What would life be like without her? She reached down and kissed her.

Yuck, that dirt really was disgusting.

Charlotte smiled up into Leila's face and let her fingers play with her coarse mane.

'Leila, you're a legend.'

She knew what Leila would be thinking. 'Duh, tell me something I don't know.'

Strudworth had been unable to get a phone signal from the car and had driven back to the highway and found a payphone from where she had called the emergency line. She had then called Joel Gold, who had been understandably shocked to learn of Sarah-Jane's staged kidnapping. He said he would get there as soon as he could. It took Strudworth around thirty minutes to make it back to the old town. She was shocked at what she found: Charlotte and Sarah-Jane looking as though they were made of ebony.

'You should be thoroughly ashamed of yourself, young lady,' she upbraided Sarah-Jane after being told the full story.

'I know. I'm so terribly sorry, I really am.'

It was nearly an hour before the rescue crew arrived by helicopter and four wheel drive, only to be told they were no longer needed. Joel Gold flew in by helicopter shortly after the rescue crew had gone. Mr Gold was shocked to learn Sarah-Jane and Charlotte had both nearly perished. Sarah-Jane seized Joel Gold by the hand.

'Please, Mr Gold, I never meant for anybody to get hurt.'

Especially not yourself, thought Leila, who was eavesdropping on the private conversation while the others took themselves off a respectable distance to enjoy the picnic hamper Mr Gold had brought with him.

'Not only could you have been killed yourself, Charlotte could have been killed.'

'I know. I'm so sorry.' Sarah-Jane was in tears.

'You owe that girl your life.'

'I know that.'

'Then there are the police. Wasting their time and resources.'

'Will they charge me with something?'

'I've got them to forego charges on the grounds you do charity work to help raise money.'

'Anything, you name it.'

Sarah-Jane was blubbering. In spite of their rivalry Leila did feel a little sympathy for her. Let's face it, she herself had made a few mistakes. That all-night party at Venice Beach when she'd had too much red cordial and wound up putting her hooves through a shop window. She'd been trying to show JLo how to do a real salsa. Then there was that other time at the promotional trip to the chocolate factory when she'd got her head stuck in the candy dispenser and they'd had to get the fire-department guys to free her.

Mr Gold had not finished admonishing Sarah-Jane. 'And what about the time delay you've caused on the movie? You know how much you've cost the studio? That's coming straight from your pay!'

'Fine.'

Elsewhere Todd and Charlotte were making short work of the picnic hamper. Miss Strudworth heaped praise on them both.

'Magnificent work. Quick thinking.'

'It was Charlotte. I didn't do much at all.'

As usual, Todd made little of his contribution.

Mr Gold advanced with Sarah-Jane.

'Sarah-Jane has something to say,' he announced.

Sarah-Jane's confidence, bordering on arrogance, had been squashed flat.

'I owe you guys my life. If there's ever anything I can do for you, please let me. I am so sorry for what I put you all through. And Charlotte, thank you for tracking me down and risking your life.'

Mr Gold nodded as if that response had passed muster.

'The media know nothing of this and I would implore you all to keep quiet about it, even though I can't stop you from talking. If you did say something it might torpedo the movie, though, and then we're all sunk.'

'I think I can safely say it stays here,' said Strudworth. Charlotte and Todd nodded.

Mr Gold rubbed his hands together. 'Very well. Let's put this behind us and make a really great movie. Charlotte, I'm going to see you and Todd get lifetime passes to Excelsior Theme Parks worldwide.'

Charlotte wasn't too sure she'd take him up on that. The last trip was still fresh in her mind.

'And I'm also going to see you both get special credits on the movie.'

Todd grinned. 'Wow, my name on screen.'

'Right now, though, we had best be getting back to work.'

Sarah-Jane was flying back with Mr Gold but Leila was happy to be sharing the float with Warrior again on the way back to L.A. They had worked pretty darn well as a team.

As Charlotte was preparing her for the float, Sarah-Jane came up to them. 'Charlotte, you're really cool. Maybe we could hang out together sometime?'

'I guess,' said Charlotte, not sure what she and Sarah-Jane would have in common.

'And Leila, I know you and I have had our differences but I really appreciate you getting me out of trouble.'

Sarah-Jane kissed her. 'I'll see you guys on set tomorrow,' she said, before leaving for the helicopter.

'Maybe she's getting some sense knocked into her after all,' said Leila, watching as it took off.

By the time they got back to Los Angeles, Charlotte was exhausted but it was Todd's last night in town and though it wasn't his first trip to L.A., he was keen for some sightseeing. In the trailer, Leila was full of suggestions.

'How about the Viper Club?'

'We're not old enough.'

'Right.' There was a long pause. 'The Whiskey!'

'Leila, it's another club.' Leila was nodding.

'Okay, hold your horses.' She sniggered at her joke. 'Just get Fernando to drive you around in the limo. Go up to the hills, drink in the stars. Then down to Santa Monica, get some sand between your toes. And hook up the float.'

'What?'

'You don't think you're going without me?'

'You have to work tomorrow.'

'You forget, rust never sleeps.'

'What does that mean?'

'I don't know but it sounds groovy. Now hook up the trailer and stick one of those radio mikes on my neck and tune it to the car's radio frequency. I'll give you the full Hollywood experience. And get a file under those nails. There's so much dirt you could plant a garden.'

After a quick shower, Charlotte did as she was told. It was easier than arguing with Leila. Miss Strudworth had decided to rest after the long day so it was just Charlotte and Fernando in front and Leila in the float as they cruised to the hotel where Todd was staying. A voice like a tour guide burst through the cabin.

'The Rendezvous Hotel. One of the most famous in Los Angeles . . .'

'What's that?' asked a surprised Fernando.

It was Leila, that's what it was. Charlotte couldn't say that, of course.

'It's an interactive voice guide.'

'Huh, amazing what they can do these days.'

'. . . The Rendezvous was the scene of the infamous milk bath in 1926 where Hollywood starlet Mimi Moccopone bathed in the foyer in a tub of milk to win publicity for her new film – *Anthony and Cleopatra*. The stunt was repeated many years later by that crazy actor, Leila. She didn't do it for publicity but on a dare from her friend Paris.'

Charlotte searched for a way to turn off the speakers but couldn't find one. They pulled to the kerb where Todd was waiting with hot dogs.

'Thought you might want to eat?' he said as he climbed in and offered a delicious-looking hot dog.

'Yum. Do I ever.'

'What about the horse in the back?' came Leila's voice.

'What's that?' Todd looked around.

'Just a little trick of mine. Don't worry. Fernando, could you take us through Beverly Hills?'

'Of course, Miss Charlotte.'

There wasn't much you could see from the road of the actual houses hidden behind hedges and gates but Leila compensated.

'This is the home of Meredith Dunlop, who starred opposite Russell Raven in *New Jersey Jerk*. Apparently after a brief romantic liaison Raven and Dunlop fought, resulting in Raven cutting off her hair with a hedge trimmer. It was a blessing in disguise for Dunlop when Leila, the amazing wonder horse, suggested from a stall of the Four Seasons ladies toilet that Dunlop should do a film of *The Cancer Dancer*, which resulted in Dunlop receiving an Academy Award nomination as a bald dancer undergoing chemotherapy.'

Todd was laughing. 'You really do have an imagination, Charlotte. Is that some tape you made?'

''Fraid so,' said Charlotte as Leila talked them through numerous similar dwellings.

From Beverly Hills they swung west to Santa Monica. Charlotte was excited when Fernando parked close to the ocean. She and Todd stepped from the car into the warm night.

She sniffed. 'What's that funny smell?'

Todd sniffed, confused. 'I can't smell anything weird.'

Charlotte sniffed again. 'It's kind of salty.'

'I think you mean the ocean,' said Todd.

'So that's what it smells like.'

'Haven't you smelled the ocean before?'

Charlotte shook her head. 'This is as close to the ocean as I've ever been.'

Todd laughed. 'Then we had better go for a paddle.'

They opened the float and Charlotte brought out Leila.

'Thought you were going to leave me in there,' she whispered. 'Love Santa Monica. Used to gallop with Pierce Brosnan pre-breakfast.'

They walked down to the beach and Charlotte took off her shoes. She was wearing her one and only summer dress, but that didn't stop her edging to the ocean, excited but afraid.

'Come on, Charlotte.'

Todd put out his hand and she took it and allowed herself to be led into the surf, up to her ankles. The water was cold and made her giggle. She was just beginning to relax when Leila galloped past and did a big lunge into the ocean, spraying her with sea water.

'Thanks, Leila. My best dress!'

But it didn't matter because the whole thing was so amazing. The ocean was definitely a lot bigger than the waterhole at Darley's Crossing. After nearly an hour of frolicking, Todd bought them whopping ice-creams.

'Where to now?' said Todd as they munched.

'How about Griffith Park Observatory?' said Leila, so carried away with the ice-cream she forgot Todd didn't know she could speak. Fortunately Todd was looking away. He turned around to see who had made the comment and assumed it was an old woman, who had jogged past carrying weights.

'Not a bad idea,' said Todd. 'Have you been there?'

Charlotte explained that though they had filmed in the Botanical Gardens, she hadn't been to the Observatory.

Todd beamed. 'It's really great fun. You can look at planets and stars. It stays open till 10 pm.'

Charlotte put Leila back in the float and gave Fernando the destination but not before she had disconnected Leila's microphone.

'Don't you like the commentary?' she'd asked, offended.

'It's really good, Leila, but it's all about you.'

'Of course, that's why it's really good.'

'You should rest your voice. You have a big day tomorrow,' said Charlotte, slamming shut the back of the float.

It was only then that Leila realised she'd been conned.

'But I don't use my voice!' she yelled too late, as Fernando swung onto the freeway.

Though it was quite a distance from the beach, the traffic was light and Fernando seemed to have a few tricks up his sleeve so it didn't take all that long. When Charlotte went to get Leila from the float, all she got as a response was loud snoring. Obviously the strenuous day had taken its toll on Leila. She decided to leave her there.

Charlotte and Todd joined groups of people who were enjoying the balmy night looking through various telescopes at the stars and moon. Some of the telescopes were as big as Leila's mirror – and that was big! Charlotte gazed up at the moon and found herself thinking that this was the very same moon she had looked up at even as a small child on the other side of the planet, in Snake Hills. Knowing that her mother, when she was alive, would have stared at it too, probably many times in Charlotte's father's arms, made her feel happy and warm, a bit like cookies and hot chocolate, only better. It was a great way to end a wonderful night.

All the same, she would be pleased to get back to Australia and see her father again and tell him all about having beach sand between her toes.

Fernando dropped Todd back at his hotel. He was leaving the next day.

'Take care, Charlotte. I'll see you back at Thornton Downs.'

'I'll look forward to it.'

It was a pity Todd couldn't stay on but she was pleased to have been able to spend even a little time with him. Back at Mr Gold's, Leila woke when Charlotte opened the float.

'Are we at Griffith Park already? Fernando should try his luck in the Indy 500.'

'We've already been to Griffith Park.'

Leila didn't believe her.

'You were asleep,' said Charlotte

'Me? No way. I'm party girl numero uno.'

But once inside the trailer, party girl numero uno literally hit the hay and went right back to sleep.

'Big day?' asked Feathers.

'You might say that,' said Charlotte.

Feathers yawned. 'Let's hope that cat turns up before they run out of script to shoot.'

In her excitement Charlotte had forgotten all about Oscar and Honey. She might have saved Sarah-Jane but that didn't mean she had saved the film.

Chapter 14

The next two days on set went really well. Sarah-Jane was a model of good behaviour and Leila responded to match her co-star. Tommy Tempest shot every scene he wanted. Unfortunately Honey, despite visiting a number of psychologists, had been unable to overcome her depression and had written not a word more. What she had already written would be finished filming within the week. Joel Gold and Hector Martinez decided they would have to employ another writer but when Leila got to peek at the new writer's script that Feathers had appropriated from Mr Gold's trailer, she announced to Charlotte, 'It sucks bad. This is going to be a disaster.'

Charlotte and Sarah-Jane had formed quite a friendship and usually ate lunch together. Charlotte was surprised to hear that Sarah-Jane's parents hadn't come to Los Angeles to see how she was.

'They're both very busy lawyers,' said Sarah-Jane.

'They'll come to the red carpet opening, of course.' Sarah-Jane said it in a way that let Charlotte know she was disappointed in them. Charlotte could never imagine her father not coming to see her if she'd got herself in trouble or done something equally stupid. She thought about what he would be doing right then, probably on a cattle muster somewhere, sleeping under the stars. What a different world to this.

Sarah-Jane had also managed to sneak a peek at the work in progress.

'Awful,' was her comment. 'If we make it, it will be a failure and my career will be over. If we don't, we're stuck anyway. Where is that cat?'

Which was exactly what Charlotte had been pondering for some time too. Charlotte took herself into the trailer and made some notes. They read:

Somebody poses as window-cleaner to steal Oscar. Why?

Annoyed at Honey? Everybody says she has no enemies.

The cat was valuable?

If Oscar was valuable, it was a good reason to steal him. But how was he valuable? He was valuable to Honey but nobody had asked her for a ransom.

Charlotte thought long and hard about it. How else was Oscar valuable? Why Oscar?

And then it came to her.

There really was only one way in which Oscar was different to any other cat. Honey needed him to write. By stealing Oscar the thief put the movie in jeopardy. Charlotte felt she was onto something. She began to look at everything she knew about the film. Even before she had arrived, somebody had run into Tommy Tempest. His leg could have been broken. But they failed and Tommy was okay to continue so they switched to plan B – Oscar.

A shiver went through Charlotte when she thought about the next piece in the puzzle; the trip to the Excelsior Theme Park. Perhaps it was not an accident that she and Leila were nearly injured or killed? Maybe somebody wanted to stop the film so badly they didn't want to rely just on Honey not being able to write. Charlotte wrote two words on her pad and smiled at them, satisfied she was correct.

ɔ ɔ ɔ ɔ

'Inside job?' chorused Feathers and Leila later in the trailer as they read what she had written.

'Exactly.' Charlotte went through her points. 'Only somebody close to the film could have been on the lot to run over Tommy. And not that many people would know where Honey Grace lived and how attached she was to Oscar. And as for us going to the theme park that night, there was probably only the immediate crew who would have known.'

'It definitely smells,' said Feathers. 'I think the kid has something.'

Leila had to concede it did make sense.

'The next question is who?' said Charlotte.

'Oh, I hope it's not Consuela,' moaned Leila. 'Her hands are divine.'

There was one thing that Charlotte wasn't clear about. 'Perhaps you guys can explain to me why somebody would want to stop the movie.'

'Money!' they chorused.

'But how? What money would anybody get?'

Leila looked at Feathers. 'You want to tell her or shall I?'

Feathers started in. 'Leila and Sarah-Jane are a huge franchise for the studio. The opposition studios are running scared this will be a big hit and sink their movies that come out at the same time. Apex Studios has another one of those animated movies about ants and bees where the loser bee becomes a hero; Neptune

Studios is doing one of those things where a kid has a magic skateboard.'

'We're talking fifty million a movie,' put in Leila.

Charlotte got the drift. 'So they might pay somebody close to this movie to sabotage it?'

'Welcome to Hollywood,' said Feathers.

'So who is the "dirty rat"?' Leila put on a movie gangster voice.

The three sat in silence for a moment. Then Charlotte said, 'I suppose we can look for somebody who is suddenly flashing money around.'

'Or has a van,' said Feathers. 'If they were pretending to be a window cleaner . . .'

'Wait a second!' Leila's voice cracked loud in the trailer. 'Of course. Mac.'

Charlotte had to think hard who Mac was. 'The man with the beard?'

'Yeah, and bad guys always have beards, right? I should have known straight off.'

'Hate to disappoint you, Leila, but just because somebody has a beard doesn't mean they are bad.'

Leila had read up on a little Australian history.

'No? What about Ned Kelly? What about Osama Bin Laden?'

'What about Santa Claus?' cracked Feathers.

Leila got in a huff. 'It's not just the beard, you scaly-legged piece of ornithology. Mac happens to be a gambler with a bad habit.'

'You mean he picks his nose?' Feathers was lost.

'No I mean he *gambles*, bird brain.'

'How do you know this?' asked Charlotte.

'How do you think? I eavesdropped.'

Leila recounted the conversations she had overheard between Mac and his bookie, in which it was clear Mac had owed the bookie big-time. Mac, however, had kept promising the bookie he had money coming.

Charlotte considered. 'He definitely said he was expecting money?'

'Yes. And he got it too.'

'And he has a van!' squawked Feathers triumphantly.

'Would he have known about Oscar?' asked Charlotte.

'Everybody on the crew knew about Oscar. Honey would always bring him to the wrap party,' said Leila.

Feathers chirped in. 'By the way, with the wrap party this time do you think you could give me a little more notice than usual?'

Leila snapped, 'I always give you notice. You nod off on your perch and forget.'

'I don't "forget" what I haven't been told.'

Charlotte had to step in. 'You two, do you mind? Mac? Money? Would he have been able to run over Tommy?'

'He spends a lot of time at the studio,' confirmed Leila.

'Let's tell Mr Gold. Get the traitor keelhauled.' There was relish in Feathers' voice.

'Keelhauled?' Leila pulled a face.

'Yeah, I was in a pirate movie once. That's how I started my career, on the shoulder of a one-legged pirate with an eye patch.'

There was a knock on the door. Zara called through. 'Leila on set in five minutes.'

'I'll do this scene. Then you go to Mr Gold,' said Leila. 'In the meantime, keep your ears and eyes open.'

Charlotte groomed Leila and walked her out to the set, trying hard to not look too closely at Mac. He seemed like a nice enough man but perhaps if he owed money he'd become desperate. Charlotte was walking back from make-up when at the back of one of the trailers she heard a man's voice.

'I've booked us first class to Paris and then on to London . . . I told you I was coming into money. You didn't believe me, did you? I just had to do a little unpleasant work first.'

The words stopped Charlotte cold. Could the man be talking about stealing Oscar? Obviously he had money to spend if he was booking first class airfares. She leaned forward to try to catch a glimpse of whoever was talking but just as she craned around and put all her weight on a stack of empty film cans, they collapsed.

'Wait a second.'

The man stopped talking. She heard steps coming towards her . . .

There was nowhere to run so she slid under the trailer. She held her breath as the man moved over to where she had been standing, and waited. Charlotte couldn't see his face but his shoes were very shiny patent leather, which none of the crew wore. After a short time the man moved off. Charlotte slid out but whoever it was had vanished. Her heart was pounding fast.

Chapter 15

'You didn't see his face?' asked Feathers later, between scenes.

'No.'

'Would you recognise his voice?'

Charlotte wasn't sure that she would. Unfortunately a lot of American men sounded the same to her. 'But I would recognise his shoes.'

'Atta girl,' chuckled Leila. 'An eye for shoes. Come on, let's get over to the coffee cart and take a look at the suspects.'

Everybody had gathered for a coffee break. Charlotte walked around, eyes on the ground, checking out shoes. There were boots, grubby sneakers, new sneakers and loafers, but only three pairs of patent leather shoes. Charlotte felt a little wriggle up her spine when she saw the ones that she had seen while hiding under the trailer. Her eyes lifted from the shoes to his face. He was talking to Zara.

Charlotte recognised him now; not very tall, with black hair. This was the same man who was being treated the other day by the nurse for scratches on his arms. He had claimed they were from brambles. But what if they were from Oscar?

Leila was just about to snaffle a fat pastry snail when she felt a jab in her ribs. She looked over, annoyed at Charlotte, who was always trying to cut out all the fun food from Leila's diet, but when Charlotte jerked her head and slid her eyes in the direction of Zara and Tommy's assistant, she remembered why they had come to the coffee cart in the first place. This must be the guy. Zara looked over and saw Charlotte staring.

'Hi Charlotte, need anything?'

Charlotte was a bit stricken. The man seemed to be eyeing her keenly. Had he caught a glimpse of her before?

Zara gestured at the suspect. 'You know Rufus?'

Charlotte found herself stammering, 'Um . . . hi.' She flashed a smile at Zara and tried desperately to find an excuse. 'Is the farrier around? I think Leila has a loose shoe.'

Zara picked up her mobile and spoke into it quickly and efficiently.

Charlotte smiled self-consciously at Rufus.

'How are your arms?' she said.

He looked at her curiously and she was forced to explain.

'The other day I saw you with the nurse.'

'Oh, right. No, they're fine now.'

Charlotte decided to push her luck. 'Those cat claws can cut quite deep.'

Listening in, Leila figured Charlotte was trying to get him off guard.

'It wasn't a cat,' he said definitely. 'Brambles. I've been working on a garden.'

Zara ended the call. 'The farrier will be at the east end by the lake waiting for you.'

Charlotte thanked them and they hustled off.

'Thanks a lot,' huffed Leila. 'Not only do I miss out on a pastry, now I get nails hammered into my hoof.'

'You don't feel it.'

'Who are you to know what I feel?' shot back Leila.

'You need new shoes anyway.'

'Well, I want the ultralight Swedish design sort that Madonna collaborated on, not something a country hack would wear.'

Charlotte ignored Leila.

'I think he's the guy,' said Charlotte. 'In fact I'm sure of it.'

Leila did not share her certainty. Rufus hadn't even blinked when a cat had been mentioned. She still liked Mac for the catnapping. She'd known a lot of gamblers in her time and they would sell their mother for a dollar. In fact there were times Leila would gladly have sold her mother for a dollar, but that was a mother–daughter thing.

'Mac has a van, remember.'

'Rufus could have hired one.'

Charlotte said she would just have to tell Mr Gold her suspicions and let him figure it out. That did not appeal to Leila.

'All my life I've wanted to do a detective movie and here we have the perfect chance and you want to just hand it over. We've done all the work. We should follow this through.'

'This isn't a movie, Leila. This is real.'

'Yeah, that's what Frangelina De Fontaine says about her lips too. Believe me, I was there. The fat they injected into her lips came from my butt. It was a win-win situation and we split the bill.'

'So what do you propose?'

'I propose we take a look at their places and see if Oscar is there.'

'What? One of these guys tried to kill us.'

Leila shrugged that off.

'We weren't prepared, now we are.' Leila didn't wait for a reply. She trotted to the production office knowing Charlotte would follow.

'What are we doing here?'

'All their addresses are on the production sheet. Go in and find where they live.'

Charlotte glared at Leila, who smiled with all her teeth.

'Please.'

Charlotte knew it was foolish but it was also quite exciting. She went in and flicked through the sheet on the wall, taking a note of where Mac and Rufus lived. Leila checked out the addresses.

'Mac is in Silverlake. That's close by. Rufus is North Hollywood, not too far. Soon as we wrap, you and me are taking a look-see.'

ɔ ɔ ɔ ɔ

Feathers was muttering as Charlotte saddled Leila up at the end of the day's shoot. 'This is madness.'

'You're just a scared tweety-bird,' laughed Leila.

'Charlotte, don't go along with it.'

Charlotte was finishing off a letter on the computer. 'I'll be very careful. Don't worry. If we don't come back, you deliver this letter to Mr Gold. I've

238

written out all our suspicions.'

Charlotte printed off the letter and hid it on top of the air-conditioning unit. Leila was champing at the bit.

'Let's go, Watson.'

Leila had seen a number of Sherlock Holmes movies and always fancied she could do as well as the lean detective in following clues. Charlotte was definitely her Watson.

It didn't take them long at all to find their way to Mac's place, a converted garage in a street adorned by motorcycles, litter and cyclone fencing. Just the kind of street where some low-life cat thief might live. Mac's van was nowhere to be seen.

'Check the garbage,' ordered Leila. 'See if there's any cat food.'

Charlotte lifted the bin lid and poked around with a stick. A lot of empty beer bottles, betting stubs and pizza cartons, but no cat food.

'Smells pretty good.' Leila flipped open the pizza cartons and found an uneaten slice. 'Gold!'

'Don't be disgusting.'

Charlotte slammed the bin lid down.

Leila nudged her. 'Let's take a peek.'

There was nobody visible in the street but Charlotte didn't like going any further than this.

'Let's not.'

A meow sounded from the back of the house. Leila wasn't waiting. Oscar was there. She would free the stupid fleabag and be a hero. Mr Gold might even give her a detective movie to star in. Leila had to squeeze down a narrow path to a backyard of dead grass, boxes of junk and an empty swimming pool.

'Oscar, is that you?' she hissed, close to the back window covered by newspaper.

'It's not Oscar.'

Charlotte had reached Leila and was pointing to a small black cat sitting on top of the back fence, hungrily eyeing off a small bird tantalisingly out of reach on the lower branch of a tree. Leila considered this was inconclusive.

'Oscar could still be inside.'

But before they could debate that, a rumbling engine approached.

Mac was back!

The van was coming up the side, blocking their escape, and the house next door was right up against the fence, preventing them jumping that way. Charlotte swung onto Leila's back in one motion and jumped her into the not quite empty swimming pool. Leila's hooves landed with a splash in the dark mucky

mix of dirt, water, leaves and . . . her nostrils didn't lie
. . . stale beer. Yuck!

Nothing short of a steam bath would get rid of that.

They listened anxiously as the engine switched
off and the car door opened. Leila caught the waft
of fried chicken and was about to smack her lips
when she noticed Charlotte's stern glance telling her
to shut up.

Mac was on the phone to somebody.

'No, I still have it. You don't think I'd get rid of it, do
you? The longer I keep it, the more it's worth.'

Leila glanced up. Mac's boots were level with
her head. If he looked this way they were history. But
Mac didn't look. He turned and walked back to
the house. They waited in the foul-smelling water for
another five minutes, then Charlotte remounted Leila.

'You got us into this mess. You can get us out.'

It was a steep jump out of the pool with not much
run-up but Leila had no intention of staying a second
longer in this muck. She cleared it easily. Mac's van
was now up the side, leaving space behind it to
squeeze back out. As soon as they were out in the
street, Leila began.

'You hear what he said? "I still have it." Obviously
he's got Oscar. If he gets rid of it, there's no guarantee
he'll get paid.'

'Or he's talking about something completely different.'

'Okay. Let's check out your prime suspect. See how the ducks line up there.'

Charlotte really didn't want to. One close call was enough for the night, but then Leila would only go on about Mac being the culprit and she was sure it was Rufus. They galloped in the direction of North Hollywood.

The apartment block where Rufus lived was in stark contrast to Mac's. Very flash with a small landscaped garden, it was in a quiet North Hollywood street. Leila had been to many a party around here. The apartment block was only three stories tall. Rufus' apartment was around the back on the ground floor.

'Not a bramble in sight,' observed Charlotte from behind the neatly trimmed hedge. Leila nodded at it.

'Nobody in this block did this. It's professional.'

As they were talking, the rear door of the block opened and Rufus appeared.

'Tommy always has a dim sum dinner at 8 pm, where his assistants have to take notes,' said Leila knowingly. 'You've got an hour, easy, before he comes back.'

'*I've* got an hour?' Charlotte wondered if she'd heard correctly.

'He's your boy,' said Leila. 'Besides, if Oscar is in there he might freak and scratch me.'

'Whereas it's okay if he scratches me?'

'Hey, no offence but you don't have to look your best for close-ups.'

'I'm not breaking into somebody's apartment.'

'You don't have to. I'll do it.'

'But . . .'

Charlotte didn't get out her protest in time. Leila trotted to the intercom and pressed every button.

'Flowers,' she announced. At least three apartments responded by clicking open the door. Leila shoved in her hoof and winked at Charlotte.

'Women don't think twice if they think somebody has sent flowers. And we haven't even broken in.'

Charlotte slid into the vestibule, still protesting.

'I refuse to break into his apartment.'

'You don't need to. Reach into my saddlebag.'

Charlotte did, emerging with a doctor's stethoscope.

'Pays to be prepared,' winked Leila. 'Put it against the door and see if you can hear anything.'

'But Oscar could be sleeping.'

'Not when I bark into the intercom. He'll think it's a dog and begin moving around.'

Charlotte never ceased to be amazed at Leila's evil

genius. She went down the hall and placed the stethoscope at the door.

Outside, Leila hit Rufus' button and was about to do a good imitation of an annoying terrier, sure to get any cat up and about, when she saw a security car pull up and a very large guard get out. Leila swallowed hard. There always had to be a fly in the ointment. The guard advanced, staring curiously at Leila.

Leila went for it. 'You have just entered a covert L.A.P.D. operation. Clear the area immediately.'

The security guard stared in disbelief. 'You can talk?'

'No, you idiot. This is central command ops. The horse's eyes are a sensitive camera. I am speaking to you via a microphone in the horse's mouth.'

'Wow.'

The security guard stood there a moment, then leaned into Leila's face. She thought he was going to kiss her, she could even smell garlic on his breath, but he obviously was trying to talk into what he thought was a microphone.

'I'd love to join the L.A.P.D. Can you put in a word for me?'

'Listen, you idiot, get out of there now or I'll have you arrested.'

The security guard scrambled to his car and roared off.

Charlotte, who had been stuck inside, listening to the exchange, came storming out.

'No more silly games. I'm going to tell Mr Gold.'

That night Charlotte nervously took herself off to Mr Gold's trailer and knocked.

'Come in.'

Charlotte entered to find Miss Strudworth and Mr Gold dining. They greeted her warmly and asked if she would like to join them. Charlotte declined.

'How can I help, Charlotte?' asked Joel Gold.

'I hope you don't mind but I've been thinking a great deal about this Oscar business . . .'

'Oh, you want to be an actress?' Mr Gold nodded. 'Tough profession but I can give you a part . . .'

'No, Oscar the cat.'

'Oh, right.'

Miss Strudworth reached across and patted Mr Gold's hand.

'Joel has been trying not to think too hard about that,' she said.

'Tomorrow is pretty much the last day of Honey's script and the new writer's stuff is terrible.'

Charlotte took a deep breath. 'I think somebody might have taken Oscar to stop the movie.'

Joel Gold's eyebrows shot up.

'There's a thought! The other studios, of course. They're trying to wreck the picture so there'll be no box-office competition.'

Charlotte speedily took them through the incidents that had begun with Tommy's injury. She then laid out her suspects, leaving out the visits she and Leila had paid earlier. After hearing about Mac, Miss Strudworth muttered.

'Never trust a gambler, my grandfather would say.'

Joel was shaking his head sadly. 'But I've known Mac for so long. He's worked so many movies for us. Rufus I don't know very well but Tommy gave him his first job. Why would he hurt Tommy?'

Miss Strudworth said she supposed it all came down to money.

'Anyway,' said Charlotte. 'I thought I should let you know.'

'I'm glad you did, Charlotte.'

Charlotte continued. 'If you ask them straight out they'll probably deny everything and get rid of any evidence.'

'Perhaps first,' suggested Strudworth, 'you could determine where they were during the times in question? If one of them has an alibi then it must be the other.'

'Great idea, Caroline,' Mr Gold snapped his fingers. 'I know for a fact that Rufus was on the studio lot when Tommy was injured because he was running around making calls for Tommy.'

Charlotte pointed out that the other important times were when Oscar went missing and when the barrel accident happened at Excelsior Studios. Mr Gold said he would get a private detective onto that.

Strudworth giggled.

'A private detective! It's like I'm in a movie.'

'Well, you're on a set,' quipped Joel Gold, and they began laughing together. When grown-ups began laughing like children, Charlotte knew it was time to go.

'We'll reconvene tomorrow morning before the shoot,' said Mr Gold. 'I'll let you know what we've discovered. And Charlotte, well done.'

That night Charlotte couldn't sleep. Had Mac or Rufus taken Oscar? Would Mr Gold be able to find him in time? She got up for a glass of water and was surprised

247

to find Leila also awake. Feathers was fast asleep on his perch.

'I'm real worried, Charlie. Tomorrow is the last day of a decent script.'

'I know. If we don't find Oscar and get Honey writing, Thornton Downs is gone.'

'That's sad, all right, but what's really tragic is that I might wind up starring in a flop.'

'Maybe the private detective will find something.'

Leila wasn't so sure. 'Maybe not. Chances are there'll be nothing conclusive.'

'What else can we do?'

Leila said, 'We can trap him. That's what we can do.'

Charlotte was immediately excited by the thought. 'How?'

'You ever watch any of those TV shows where they use science to track the killer . . . no, that's right, you guys don't have TV in Snake Hills.'

'I'm only allowed to watch PG anyway,' said Charlotte.

'Well, take it from me, the cops these days can find the tiniest trace of whether somebody was in a car or a house.'

Charlotte was following the idea.

'But you can't just walk into somebody's house and do tests, can you?'

Leila had watched enough police TV shows to understand how it worked.

'No, you need a warrant, which is an order from a judge saying they have to let you in. And to get that you would need more evidence than we have. What I'm talking about is getting them to lead us to Oscar.'

'And how are we supposed to do that?'

Leila chuckled. 'We trick them, of course.'

Chapter 16

The next morning Charlotte entered Mr Gold's trailer to find him downcast. Miss Strudworth told Charlotte that the private detective had quickly established that Mac had been at the studio lot when Tommy had been run over. They already knew Rufus had been. The day Oscar had gone missing both men had the opportunity to take him. The night of the Excelsior Studio incident both men were nearby, Rufus allegedly doing work at the office but without anybody to alibi him, and Mac helping out on a TV shoot but with the opportunity to have snuck off.

'In short, it could be either of them,' muttered Joel Gold.

'You could go to their homes on some pretext,' said Miss Strudworth. 'See if there's any evidence of Oscar.'

Mr Gold said he'd suggested as much to the private detective.

'Trouble is, if Oscar is being held elsewhere, it might only tip them off.'

'I have an idea how we could catch them,' Charlotte offered. The idea, of course, having been Leila's, not hers.

'Pray tell,' said Miss Strudworth.

'You gather the crew at the studio tonight and tell them Oscar has been found. You say that it is almost certain he was being held nearby to where he was found and that tests will be able to show which apartment or house he was in.'

Mr Gold brightened. 'Good old forensics! Yes.'

'But we don't have Oscar,' pointed out Strudworth. Joel Gold's spirits fell.

'Nobody will know that. You just say that police will investigate all houses and apartments nearby.'

Strudworth was nodding appreciatively. 'We see who makes a break to clean up the evidence. Whichever one leaves is our saboteur. I'm surprised, Richards, I didn't think you had this much deceit in you.'

Charlotte smiled as best she could. She couldn't very well say it was all Leila's idea.

Joel Gold clapped his hands together.

'We'll set up a meeting at the studio and order all the crew there. I love this girl. We're going to make this movie after all.'

Leila had never experienced anything like the strange vibe in the air as the day's shoot progressed. Things went without major problems; people did their jobs; Sarah-Jane continued her good behaviour and even shared a piece of her salad roll with Leila. Yet everybody knew that either the movie would be postponed indefinitely or they would have to turn up and work on something less than the best. Cassandra restricted herself to just two danishes. When Tommy Tempest called wrap, the atmosphere was almost unreal. Then Mr Gold came forward and thanked everybody for their efforts so far.

'I know you are all waiting to see what we're doing with this picture. We will be announcing plans at the studio at 6 pm. Please be there.'

A buzz went through the crowd. Leila kept her eyes on both Rufus and Mac but they merely seemed as surprised as everybody else. Charlotte sidled up to her.

'One of them is a very cool customer.'

'Yep. And selfish too. All these people waiting to find out if they're still working and our saboteur couldn't care less.'

They clammed up as Sarah-Jane came striding over. She had been very busy in the last few days and Charlotte had not had much chance to talk with her except for a few words now and again during a hot chocolate break.

'Hi, Charlotte. In case they can the movie and I don't get another chance, I just wanted to thank you again for everything.'

'That's okay.'

Sarah-Jane handed over her sports bag. It felt extremely heavy.

'For you,' she said. 'You wouldn't believe the amount of free products I get sent. Lip-gloss, sunscreens, shampoo, perfume. You name it.'

Charlotte was thrilled.

'This time next week you might be back at that riding school of yours,' said Sarah-Jane. 'Think of me when you wash your hair.'

Charlotte explained that there might not be a riding school this time next week. She told Sarah-Jane all about how the lawyer father of one of the painful girls, Lucinda, was suing Miss Strudworth over her breaking a collarbone.

Sarah-Jane, a daughter of lawyers herself, listened attentively. 'Sounds like she needs a good talking to.'

'She wouldn't listen,' said Charlotte.

'Might depend on who's talking. Most girls want to be an actor like me. You know if this Lucinda has those kind of ambitions?'

Charlotte had heard her going on many times about how she would love to star in movies. 'Her friend Emma's father is some big producer and to be honest I suspect that's why Lucinda hangs out with her. Emma is even more painful than Lucinda.'

Sarah-Jane nodded. 'Miss Strudworth would have the family's details, right?'

Charlotte was confused. 'Of course.'

'Sarah-Jane?'

Tommy was calling her over. She hugged Charlotte. 'Take care.'

And then she was gone.

'Why did she want to know about Lucinda?' asked Charlotte of Leila.

'Probably wants to compare witch notes.'

'Come on, give her a break – and no, no comment about how you'd gladly break her neck. Admit it, you need Sarah-Jane and she needs you.'

'She needs me more.'

'Whatever,' said Charlotte. She was more focused on what might happen tonight.

Feathers came in and landed on Charlotte's shoulder. 'Has anybody told Honey?'

Charlotte's stomach dropped. No, they hadn't. She would have to be brought in on the plan. Charlotte found Joel Gold immediately and explained the problem. He agreed Honey had to be told.

'Can you do it, Charlotte? She likes you and I have so much to do between now and six. Fernando can take you.'

ↄ ↄ ↄ ↄ

Honey was pleased to see Charlotte, though it was clear from her red eyes and pasty face that she had been crying and not eating well.

'I've been to three psychologists but they're no use. They all want me to accept that Oscar is gone, and I don't believe that, I really don't.'

Good, thought Charlotte, perhaps she could make others think that too. She explained what they were planning. It took some time for it to sink in.

'You want me to pretend that Oscar is back with me?'

'It might be best if you simply don't answer the phone. But if you bump into somebody, just act like you're excited he's been found.'

Honey wasn't sure she could act happy at the moment.

'If you really want Oscar back, you'll do it.'

Honey steeled herself. 'In that case, I'll give an "Oscar"-winning performance.'

Charlotte had just enough time to share a lemonade, get back to Mr Gold's, where the trailer had been towed, and get changed.

'This is it, guys,' said Leila.

She lifted her hoof for a high five. Charlotte gave skin and Feathers, feathers.

ɔ ɔ ɔ ɔ

At 6 pm the crew, cast and studio executives filed into an empty studio building on the Excelsior lot. Leila was considered part of the cast and was led in by Charlotte. Hector Martinez asked Joel Gold what was going on.

'Yes, what's going on, Joel?' echoed Hawthorn.

'I'll explain in a minute.'

Mr Gold had kept them in the dark, along with everybody else. He didn't want anybody getting wind of the 'news' until he gave it. It would be a disaster if Mac or Rufus had a chance to slip away without being observed. Joel Gold checked his watch. It was time. Fernando was outside in the car, the engine running. Joel Gold stepped forward.

'I have some good news. The movie will go on.'

An excited murmur ran through the crowd.

Mr Gold continued. 'But better than that. Honey Grace has already begun to write because Oscar has been found.'

There were gasps of surprise, whistles and applause. Mr Gold continued.

'I can't reveal the location where Oscar was found but the police assure me it is likely Oscar was being held nearby. They will be checking all houses and apartments in the immediate vicinity for traces of exactly where. The culprit will be found and the trace evidence will send them to prison for a long time.'

Charlotte kept her eyes on the suspects but neither showed great alarm. In fact they nodded at the suggestion somebody offered that the culprit should be hanged. One of them was an accomplished actor.

'So we'll see you all on set tomorrow. Now I would like you all to stick around for supper. On me.'

There was applause and whoops. Mr Gold had said that nobody ever knocked back a free supper, so whoever left the building would be the culprit.

'Don't you dare eat more than one apple pie,' Charlotte ordered Leila. 'Feathers, keep an eye on her.'

Then she raced outside with Mr Gold and Miss Strudworth. With high expectations they piled into

Mr Gold's car. Fernando sat ready behind the wheel.

'Fingers crossed,' said Mr Gold.

They didn't have to wait long. Almost immediately, Mac came hustling out of the building and went for his van.

'Mac. I wouldn't have believed it,' said Mr Gold bitterly. Mac pulled out and Fernando slipped in behind him. There was a crew shooting a TV show on the lot and just as Mac slipped through, a man came out and put a stop sign on them. Charlotte wanted to scream. The car was held up for an anxious minute.

'This is all we need,' muttered Joel Gold.

'Don't worry, Mr Gold, Fernando will catch him,' said the driver. As soon as they were waved through, Fernando hit the gas. Charlotte felt her body pushed back into the seat at the acceleration.

ↄ ↄ ↄ ↄ

Back in the building Leila and Feathers watched as Mac slipped quietly out the door when he thought nobody was watching.

'Said it was him all along,' whispered Leila to Feathers. 'Never trust a gambler.'

Leila turned her attention to the apple pies.

'Never trust a director's assistant either.'

Leila looked up to see what Feathers was referring to. Rufus was making a move too.

'NO! They've followed Mac. You'll have to follow him.'

'What?' shrieked Feathers. Fortunately the sound system was pumping and nobody heard.

'Traffic will be slow. You can follow from above. He's only a stone's throw away in North Hollywood anyway.'

'You ever heard of hawks!'

'Fine. I'll let the cute macaw know what a brave guy you are.'

'Okay, okay. I'll do it.'

Feathers shot out of the building just as Rufus climbed into his car and fired it up.

In Mr Gold's car, Charlotte watched anxiously as Mac's van cut and weaved among the freeway traffic. Fernando was a skilled driver and had managed to catch Mac not too far from the studio.

'He's heading towards Silverlake, where he lives,' announced Mr Gold, unaware that Charlotte had been there once herself. But then Mac turned west, not east, and was soon back in Hollywood.

'Perhaps he's keeping Oscar somewhere else.' There was more than a hint of hope in Strudworth's voice. But the hope was soon dashed when Mac pulled over in front of a small shop and rushed inside.

'I know this place,' said Fernando. 'It is a betting shop.'

Charlotte's heart fell. Mac emerged a few minutes later with a huge smile on his face, counting cash.

'Looks like he's a winner,' said Mr Gold bitterly. Mac jumped into his van, turned and headed back the way he had come. Back to the studio for a free feed.

ↄ ↄ ↄ ↄ

Feathers was out of condition for this kind of effort. It was still light enough to clearly spy Rufus' electric blue car below and there was enough traffic to allow Feathers to catch up. He glided whenever he could and at North Hollywood, he breathed a sigh of relief. But it soon turned to panic. Rufus continued up into the Hollywood Hills – hawk and other angry bird territory. Feathers was tempted to turn back but he owed Mr Gold so he stuck at it. On one of the high roads that overlooked L.A., Rufus pulled into a house. Feathers dropped like a stone, panting with relief. The house was old and ramshackle. Just the sort of place to stash a stolen cat. Rufus went into a garage and changed clothes, emerging in overalls. Hmm, what was he up to? Feathers shivered when he saw Rufus producing a long-handled shovel. Oh, no! Was he digging a grave for Oscar? Even though it was a cat, the most deadly enemy a bird could have, Feathers felt sorry for it. Oscar had sounded like he was one of those good cats. And now he was to be killed and buried! Rufus, however, kept digging, long after what he needed for a simple cat grave. Then he went back into the shed and came out with boxes of seedlings. The guy was gardening!

‌⌒ ⌒ ⌒

'A complete bust,' said Leila back at the studio. Feathers was on his third tall glass of choc-milk, Charlotte was upset. She didn't know how she was going to tell Honey that the ruse hadn't worked.

'So what was the story with Rufus?' asked Leila.

Charlotte relayed what she knew. 'Mr Gold made some enquiries. An aunt died and left him a run-down house in the hills. That's how he had money for first class airfares. He's been cleaning up the house. He was telling the truth about the brambles.'

Leila grunted. 'So you were wrong, Charlie. This sucks.'

'I was wrong?'

'It was your idea that somebody was trying to torpedo the movie.'

'And I still think that makes sense.' She thought for a moment. 'Did anybody else leave the supper?'

Feathers shrugged. 'I left right after Rufus.'

Leila shrugged. Once Feathers had gone, she hadn't paid attention to anything but apple pies.

Charlotte had an idea. 'There was a TV crew shooting outside. Maybe they caught something on film?'

Charlotte didn't want to go to Mr Gold unless she had something concrete, so she took it on herself. She gathered up all the food and cake she could find, mounted Leila and went looking for the TV crew.

It was good timing. They were breaking for coffee.

'Hey, it's Leila!' called out a girl with a heap of stopwatches around her neck.

'Thought you guys might like some yummy food,' said Charlotte, offering the bag.

'I know you. You're Crocodoll Dundee. Loved that thing with the snakes,' said a big guy.

'Actually, I need a bit of a favour,' said Charlotte as the crew checked out the goodies on offer. 'You guys were shooting near the studio shed and I really need to see if you caught something on film.'

'Ask Monica,' said the big guy, pointing at a blonde girl.

'Sure. Come and have a look,' said Monica after Charlotte had given her request. She led Charlotte to where a monitor was set up. 'It's all time coded.'

Charlotte said she needed from six to six-forty, and Monica found the camera shots that corresponded. Charlotte and Leila watched with beating hearts. One of the camera shots found cars as they approached the point where Fernando had been stopped. There was Mac in his van, followed by Mr Gold's limo. A couple of minutes later, Rufus sped through. And then a minute after that, there was one more car. Leila didn't recognise the car but she recognised the driver.

It was Hawthorn.

Chapter 17

Hawthorn. Of course! He was right on the spot when they had gone on the tour and nearly been killed. He was the one who had been entrusted to find who had run over Tommy and had claimed to find nobody. That was because it was him! Charlotte and Leila galloped back to the studio to inform Joel Gold, only to be told by Feathers that he had gone to give Hector Martinez the bad news that everything he had said earlier had been a lie.

'We can't wait,' said Leila. 'Once Hawthorn knows Oscar wasn't found, he'll begin destroying evidence. Maybe starting with Oscar.'

Charlotte saw Zara lurking and ran to her.

'Would you know where Hawthorn lives, by any chance?'

Zara flicked through her Palm Pilot.

'3467 Almeda. It's only a couple of miles south.'

Charlotte didn't bother to explain why she'd asked.

She ran back to Leila and mounted her, yelling the address.

Leila knew the area well. A lot of the studio execs lived nearby and Leila had been guest of honour at many of their kids' parties. They galloped to the gate, not bothering to wait for the guard to open it. Charlotte dug in her knees and Leila leapt, clearing it easily.

'What's the quickest route?' called Charlotte.

'We don't want to take that, believe me,' yelled Leila.

'Yes, we do.'

'Okay then, but you asked for it.'

Leila veered across the six-lane freeway, just avoiding a speeding Corvette and nipping between a light truck and a rushing Olds. Horns blared.

'This is the quickest route?' yelled Charlotte.

'Yep.'

Leila powered across to the other side of the freeway. The traffic was now coming from the opposite direction. Things were going well until they found themselves heading for a collision with a speeding motorcycle. If they slowed they would be cleaned up by a fast approaching Mercedes. Leila took the only option available, she jumped. They cleared the startled biker and landed in scrub on the side of the freeway.

From here it was all downhill, literally. Leila was galloping fast as she turned into Almeda and sped towards the block where Hawthorn lived. They were just in time. Wearing rubber gloves, Hawthorn was heading to his car holding a pillowslip that was writhing. A high-pitched meow indicated it was Oscar.

'Put Oscar down,' yelled Charlotte.

Hawthorn turned at the words. His face contorted in surprise. 'You!'

'Put him down.'

'And you're going to make me?'

Charlotte wasn't certain what to do next. Hawthorn smiled, sure of himself.

'You try to stop me, the cat gets it.'

Charlotte was frozen. So near and yet so . . .

Wham!

Something plummeted from the sky and smacked Hawthorn in the face. He let out a scream as scaly claws seized his cheeks and a hooked beak bit his nose.

Feathers to the rescue!

Hawthorn dropped the bag and a hissing ball of fur erupted and began lashing Hawthorn with sharp claws. Charlotte had never seen a cat and bird working so harmoniously.

'Please, get them off me,' yelled the flailing Hawthorn.

'I don't know why I should. You tried to kill me and Leila at the theme park.'

'Not kill you, just make sure Leila couldn't perform . . . a little insurance . . . Aeeee!' He let out another scream of pain. Charlotte now had the rope she used for runaway steers ready in her hand.

'Why?' asked Charlotte.

'Hector didn't have the confidence of the board. If the movie failed I'd be the next studio boss.'

'Okay, leave him be, Feathers,' said Charlotte.

Feathers desisted. Hawthorn took the opportunity to throw Oscar from his neck, then tried to make a run for it, but for Charlotte he was pathetically easy quarry. She twirled her lasso over her head, let it go with perfect judgement and pulled tight, leaving Hawthorn thrashing on the ground.

ᗡ ᗡ ᗡ ᗡ

By the time Charlotte, accompanied by Miss Strudworth, had given a statement to the police and returned to Mr Gold's, it was nearly midnight. She found a massive hot chocolate waiting for her and her favourite dish, shepherd's pie, which the chef,

Nunzio, had never cooked before but had done especially for her. Honey was waiting for her too, with Joel Gold. She cradled a grateful Oscar in her arms.

'I can't tell you how happy I am, Charlotte,' said Honey. 'If there's anything I can ever do for you, just ask.'

'Write the rest of the script,' suggested Charlotte.

'I'll be heading straight back home now. I've told Mr Gold that he'll have four new scenes ready for shooting tomorrow.'

Joel Gold stood with Charlotte, watching Honey Grace drive away.

'I gotta tell you, Charlotte, any time you want a job, you've got one. You saved Hector's neck. And mine.'

Charlotte pointed out that there was a little self-interest at stake.

'If the movie isn't made, Miss Strudworth doesn't get her money, and Leila and I love Thornton Downs.'

'Actually,' said Joel Gold guiding them back inside, 'Caroline might have some news on that front. But I'll let her tell you herself in the morning.'

Charlotte returned to the trailer where Leila and Feathers were still on a high, reliving the moments of Hawthorn's capture.

'Did you like my little manoeuvre?' Feathers' chest was puffed out. 'We parrots call it the talon to the melon.'

'Very nice, but I had to leap a speeding Harley Hog.'

'A motorcycle. It's not like it was a semi. It doesn't compare with plummeting out of the sky like an arrow.'

'Guys,' said Charlotte, getting in before it became a slanging match. 'I think we all did really well. I'm proud of you.'

Leila heard where she was coming from.

'We're proud of you too. It's just a shame you're not old enough to come to The Whiskey. It'll just be getting under way now.'

ↄ ↄ ↄ ↄ

'It's amazing,' blurted Strudworth. 'Out of the blue! Lucinda's father rang me to say that he was dropping the legal action.'

They were eating breakfast on the terrace.

'Did he say why?'

'No. He just said he realised I wasn't responsible for the accident. "Accident." That's the word he used. But Mr Gold will still give me the million-dollar fee, which means I can give Thornton Downs the upgrade it deserves.'

At the shoot an hour later, Charlotte located Sarah-Jane at the make-up trailer.

'Did you make a call to Lucinda?'

Sarah-Jane smirked. 'I might have rung and suggested that if she ever wanted to make it on the big screen she had better not mess with my pals.'

Who would have thought it? Sarah-Jane was going in to bat for them.

'It was the least I could do after you saved my life,' added Sarah-Jane. 'But I might have one favour to ask.'

Charlotte waited.

'If the film is a success, can you bring Leila back for another?'

'That,' said Charlotte, 'is going to be up to her.'

Chapter 18

The remaining four weeks of shooting went well. Honey delivered a great script and Leila and Sarah-Jane behaved themselves. When shooting finished, the studio threw a huge party. Leila made Charlotte shop for a new dress, a simple but elegant number that Mr Gold paid for. A very famous band played and Mr Gold danced wildly with Miss Strudworth. Leila strutted her stuff and even danced with Sarah-Jane. Charlotte and Feathers enjoyed themselves watching the others party, Charlotte wishing that Todd had still been there to dance with but happy to watch the others having fun. Sweating from her exertion, Leila came over and stuck her head in the ice fountain, which featured a carving of her own head in ice.

'Talk about hot to trot,' she muttered. She realised that a year off the party circuit had lowered her stamina.

'I might go home,' said Charlotte. She was feeling tired and the plane left the next day.

'No way, Charlie. You can't leave me.'

But Charlotte was growing weary.

'Okay then, what about one last ride up into the Hills?'

That, Charlotte could handle. They left Feathers in his cage and snuck out the back, taking their time to work their way up the hills overlooking L.A. For once the smog had cleared and the lights that glittered below were exciting and pretty.

Leila began to choke up. 'Ain't it pretty?'

Charlotte could see how much Leila loved L.A. Even though it made her heart heavy she felt she owed it to her friend to speak what was on her mind.

'I know how much you love it here. This is your home and I know I'd never want to say goodbye to my home. If you want, you can stay. I'll convince Strudworth.'

Leila teared up. 'I do love it here, Charlie. I love being a star and Consuela's pedicure and Cassandra's pastries and the giant TV . . .'

'And Feathers,' added Charlotte.

'Yeah, I guess, but more the TV. And thank you . . . I know how hard that is for you to say and yes, I do want to stay.'

Charlotte felt her heart burst.

'But,' added Leila, 'it would be harder for me to leave you. And you offering me that choice, that's the clincher. To everybody else I'm a horse. A smart horse, a very attractive horse but just a horse. Or at most just another star. But with you, I'm a friend. That means more to me than anything.'

Charlotte couldn't help tearing up. Leila ran on.

'Besides. We've got that jump-off against Milthorp in two weeks and I am going to make that arrogant fat-head Warrior eat my dust. Now, let's get back to the party for the cake.'

The two friends started back into the darkness. The moon and stars above lighting their way, their voices floating on the breeze.

'Okay, but no more of those mini pizzas.'

'Come on, I'm giving up Hollywood. Least you can let me break my diet.'

'Fine. But no cake . . .'

'No cake! What is this? Prison camp?'

Acknowledgements

A great many hardworking hands helped groom Charlotte and Leila for Hollywood. In particular I would like to thank publisher Zoe Walton, editor Chris Kunz, and all those at Random House who have nurtured these two in their three adventures. Thanks also to my agents, Fiona Inglis and Rick Raftos, for their time and support.

My family deserves special mention – Violet and Venice, for not only inspiring me to write about a girl and her special horse, but also for their feedback at each stage of the book, and young Gustavus, for keeping a smile on my face. Of course, none of this would be possible without my wife, Nicole, who gives her all every day to allow me to turn imagination into reality.

COLLECT THE SERIES

Horse Crazy & Horse Shy

Horse Sense & Horse Power

Trail Mates & Dude Ranch

Horse Play & Horse Show

Hoof Beat & Riding Camp

Horse Wise & Cade Blue

Starlight Christmas & Sea Horse

Team Play & Horse Games

Horsenapped & Pack Trip

Rachel & Rainbow

Eastabures & Fanhoot